# ANGEL IN THE SHADOWS

## Lisa Grace

Eloquent Books

Eloquent Books
An imprint of Strategic Book Group
P.O. Box 333
Durham, CT 06422
www.StrategicBookGroup.com

ISBN: 978-1-60911-001-7

Printed in the United States of America

I give all the glory to God for giving me the idea to write these books. Also, I love and appreciate my husband, Todd, who worked as my first editor, and my precious daughter, Cammy, for listening. Also, thank you to my Mom, Marge, and Dad, Ray, who always encourage me.

Last but not least, thank you to all the mighty men of God, workers and volunteers who work in the many forms of ministry, battling against evil spirits every day. Keep up the good fight.

*For by grace are ye saved through faith; and that not of yourselves: it is the gift of God: Not of works, lest any man should boast. Ephesians 2: 8–9, of the King James Bible*

# Acknowledgments

Thank you to all the people behind the scenes who bring a book to the shelves; especially the wonderful people at Strategic Book Group, including Ellen Green, Dawn Monclova, Kira Robbins, Wendy Baker, Georgie, Matthew Land, Brigitte Surette, Laura M., Joanne, James and Sherry. I would like to extend a special thank you to Tim and Wendy Boone and also Pastor Larry and JoAnne Vasseur for their words of wisdom and advice. Also, thank you to all my former students; it was a pleasure working with you. Finally, thank you to my family and friends for all their love and support.

# Contents

*. . . concerning spiritual gifts . . . I would not have you ignorant . . . to another the discerning of spirits . . . 1 Corinthians 12: 1—10, King James Bible*

# Chapter One

## Megan

Who would believe there is something different about me? No one. Most days I wake up late, move half-dazed, until mom yells she's going to leave without me; an idle threat that doesn't work.

I grab a cup of coffee, my not so secret vice, to wake me up and shift my brain in to first gear. I get to school, carrying too many AP books to make me 'in'. Anyway, you get the idea. I, Megan am a good kid leading a normal boring life in the suburban beach town of Clearwater, Florida. Then this last summer, at camp, I had a paradigm shift; (that should make Mrs. Grey my AP creative writing teacher happy) I would show this to her, but she would totally flip and make me get counseling if she suspects that I believe anything I've written is true. My world now is upside down and inside out. Let me take you back to this summer when I found out what Zadok is and who I am or might be.

*   *   *

I can't lie. I'm excited to be on our way. On the way to the lake, I see flashes of light in three or four of the cars we pass. I shake my head and I wonder if I need glasses. As we drive through the small town that borders the main road to camp, our bus stops at a red light. I notice a dark figure in the woods and squint out the window for a better look. I have no idea what I'm seeing. By the time I get one of the other kids to look, we are on our way again and what ever it was, is out of sight. I make up my mind, once I'm back home, I'm getting my eyes checked.

Finally, after a grueling eight-hour bus ride, we arrive at camp. My voice is almost gone from leading the last few hours of songs and games.

It's exciting to finally be old enough to be here as a junior camp counselor. I don't have to sneak my coffee anymore. I can go right into the counselor room and get it.

I'm bouncing with excitement because Seth and his bus should be arriving in the next two hours. We've always liked each other. Seth is so cute with light brown hair and golden brown eyes. We've been texting each other, but it'll be great to see him. We're not allowed to bring cell phones, ipods or anything to camp. There's no place to plug them in and zero reception anyway. It's about as rugged as I want to get.

"Hey Megan, help those kids get their gear and lead 'em up to check in, would ya?" Mr. Steve calls out as he steps off the bus and stretches his legs. All the kids love Mr. Steve; he's always laughing and has a smile on his face. He's kind of like the Uncle, you always wished you had.

"Sure," I say, as I'm tackled by Nikki, one of my youngsters.

"Don't worry Megan we'll help you," Nikki says as she's squeezing the life out of me. "Just grab your bags and help some of the younger kids with theirs, Okay?" I say as I peel her arms off me.

"Can I be in your cabin please, please, please, please?" Nikki asks. Secretly I'm flattered. "It's not up to me. We have to go to check in and see where we're assigned." I grab my duffle and head up the walk yelling, "This way everybody!"

Carrie, one of the other counselors is still helping some of the younger ones unload their bags from the lower storage bays on the bus. Carrie always wears her blonde hair in pigtails, even though she's the same age I am. Carrie's a total tomboy; we go to the same high school and church, but don't know each other well because we're so different. She turns to me and yells, "Go ahead I'll handle the stragglers."

The lake is peeking through the trees on the left, and I can smell the water. I'm so happy to be here, you can't wipe the smile off my face. Seth and I should be able to sneak some alone time. We have our own secret place on the lake. There's a small cliff only about eight feet high with a rotting dock about two feet down. When you sit there, you're kind of hidden from the world. Last year we would head up there and talk. You can see a million stars at night. We would count the shooting stars and satellites, while the waves lapping at the rocky shoreline, provided a rhythmic drumbeat to our senses. The bats would appear, like shadows, swooping over the lake to eat the bugs. It's mysterious and magical. You feel anything could happen at any moment. It's so nice to have someone as special as Seth and a private place to share with him.

Half the kids are racing ahead. They've been here before and are eager to show the newbies the way. The walkway leads up to the main lodge, a hulking two-story building built of log timbers and stone. Check-in is in the lobby, where it is cooler, since even in North Carolina it's humid and hot in July. The adults running the place, the Timmons, prefer not to sweat if they don't have to. There are two dormers upstairs for the youngest kids and cabins surrounding the lake for the older ones.

I wait off to the side as my young charges find out where they're assigned. I feel a quick tap on my shoulder. I turn around and see a smiling Mr. Z.

"Mr. Z.!" I give him a quick hug. "I'm so glad to see you!" Last year he was one of my favorite camp staffers.

"Megan, it's nice to see you too. I'm glad you came back to help us out. We need some staff that can chase down the young ruffians, tackle 'em, tie 'em up and keep them in line. Speaking of staff, here's your badge of courage."

I laugh as he hands me my name badge. I look at it, 'Megan Laughlin', Clearwater, FL, STAFF. I know it's kind of hokey, but I feel happy all over again.

"You know, by putting this on you become an official target for every water balloon, frog, snake and prank these kids can dream up." Mr. Z. is smiling as he speaks then I notice he seems to be glowing. What I thought was the sun behind him, isn't. It's definitely him.

I laugh and shake my head, trying to ignore what I'm seeing. "Yeah, I know I'm in for it." I pause, and just look at Mr. Z. and the aura surrounding him; then quickly look around realizing no one else in the room is seeing the glow but me.

"Are you O. K. Mr. Z.?" I ask.

"Never better Megan, why don't you find out what cabin you're in and when things calm down, we'll have some time to go over a few things."

At that moment, the main lodge door slams shut, grabbing my attention. When I look back at Mr. Z., he's gone. I know it's not normal to see people glowing. Maybe I need to cut down on the caffeine. With a jolt, a chilling thought hits me; maybe I have a brain tumor. I calm down as I look around; I realize there can't be any thing wrong with me, because no one else is looking like they walked out of some cheap 1950's movie about radiation poisoning. No one else has an aura, only Mr. Z.

Nikki, Paul and a few other youngsters, interrupt my thoughts, anxious for me to get my cabin assignment. They drag me to the check-in table.

Nikki grabs my arm and says, "We're not in the same cabin, but guess what?" Nikki's pouty face lasts for about one second over this bad news. Then she points, "See that cute boy over there? He's in the cabin next to mine an' he's going to help me carry my bags; isn't he cute!"

I ask her, "Did you notice anything strange about Mr. Z.?"

"Who's that?" She asks, never taking her eyes off the cute boy.

"The adult I was just talking to," I respond.

"No. I kinda remember him from last year, he's nice," She answers as she waves to the cute boy. "I gotta go, see you Meg," Nikki picks up her stuff and heads over to her new Romeo.

At check in, Toby one of the older counselors, with sandy blond hair, hands me a folder with the scheduled activities I'll be supervising.

"You know how to swim?" he asks.

"Yes."

"Up to date on CPR certification?" He starts checking things off on a list.

"Sure thing," I smile.

"Good. 'Cause you're assigned to lake swim duty, from 10 to 12 each day."

Then with the rapid delivery of a drill Sergeant, he checks off on his list and reads aloud, "Reveille at 7, (I groan), breakfast 7:30–9, 9–10 chapel, first swim 10–11, 2nd swim 11–12, lunch 12–1: 30, free time till 2, 2–3 First craft period, 3–4 2nd craft period, 4–5 kitchen cooking duty, 5–6:30 dinner, 6:30–7, free time, 7–8 evening chapel, 8–9:30 campfire sing along, 10 lights out. Any Questions?" I shake my head no.

"Good. Counselor meeting tonight at six-thirty. See you there."

"Yes sir!" I reply and give Toby a military salute.

He rewards me with a brief smile and a chuckle and hands me my STAFF shirt, "See ya at the meeting, Megan."

My cabin is the seventh on the left, next to the last one. When I open the screen door, I see the old familiar three sets of bunk beds, my cot, one nightstand (for me), one six-drawer dresser (one drawer for each kid) and a small communal desk. My home-sweet-home for the next eight days. I notice a small blonde girl wearing glasses already occupies the top right bunk. She is peering over the edge, watching me.

"Hi. My name is Megan, what's yours?"

"Allison."

"Is this your first time at camp?" Allison looks like she's going to cry.

"Yes."

"Well, we're going to have fun. Can you help me unpack?"

"Sure." Allison climbs down quickly from the bunk and walks over to where I'm unzipping my duffle on my cot.

"Where are you from?" I ask.

"Jacksonville. By the river."

"Nice. It's beautiful up there. Can you keep a secret?" I ask as I reach into my bag.

"Yes." Allison says earnestly.

"Good. I brought a bag of candy bracelets and you're in charge of handing them out to the rest of our cabin." I hand her the bag and Allison gives me a big smile.

I look around and notice two other bags stowed under one set of bunk beds. "Allison do you know the girls who brought those bags?"

Allison nods her head and looks excited to give me an answer, "Their names are Tasha and Tynekwa Taylor. They're twins. They seem really nice. They went to explore the camp. They invited me along, but I was to shy to go."

"Would you mind finding them and telling them I'm here. Also, don't forget to tell them about the surprise."

"Oh I won't," Allison replies. She puts the bag of bracelets on her top bunk by her pillow and starts heading out the door.

"Allison, if you see anybody looking lonely, could you do me a favor and say hello, and invite them to sit with us tonight at the campfire?"

She hesitates, turns and says, "Yes, I can do that," the door slams loudly as she hops down the steps and heads toward the beach campfire area where many of the kids are hanging out.

I smile to myself. I want my cabin kids to have a great time. Just not at my expense. Last year, I hid a snake in my counselor's desk drawer. Hopefully, my girls will be afraid of snakes and I won't find any hidden in my cot. Other than that, I think I'm ready to handle just about anything. I enjoy unpacking in peace before the rest of the kids find our cabin. It gives me a chance to think about Mr. Z. A memory keeps nudging around in my brain. Then I remember. Last year at camp, I think I saw him shining too.

A memory floods into my mind. I remember saying to him the last night of camp, "Mr. Z. you're my angel. You shine just like an angel." The other campers laughed and teased me about it; so I dropped it and avoided Mr. Z., except to say a quick goodbye the next day.

Now it was happening again. What can it mean? Why would he glow and not others? Lost in thought, I jump as I hear the cabin door swing open.

"Megan."

It's Seth.

"Seth!" I fly over to him and give him a big hug. We could get in trouble for this, but I'm so happy to see him I don't think. He smells so good, like shampoo, I don't want to let go. Seth runs his fingers through my hair and inhales deeply. I feel his heart pounding in his chest. We pull apart, a little self-consciously, amazed at our feelings.

"It's so good to see you!" I gush.

"Eight whole days together, it's going to be great," Seth smiles and reaches for my hands.

We stand there for a minute, hypnotized by our feelings. The door opens again and three more girls enter the cabin. We let go and look at the new arrivals. Seth turns to me and says, "Oh no, you're in for it now, Megan. This is Ashley," Seth says pointing to a cute brunette with short curly hair, "Brianna," pointing to a long dark brown haired girl with bangs, "and Kayla," who has golden curls and big blue eyes.

"Hi Megan, where should we put our stuff?" Ashley asks. Brianna yells out, "Dibs on a top bunk!" "I don't care which is mine," Kayla interjects as I point out the available bunks.

Seth continues his intro, "They all go to my church, watch out they're terrors."

"HA, HA," Brianna smiles sweetly batting her eye lashes. "Only to you."

"Bri is Robby's sis." Seth looks at me with a knowing smile and winks. Robby is Seth's best friend, very out going and prone to pulling pranks on people.

At that moment, Robby charges in, grabs me around the waist and twirls me around. "Did you miss me? Don't worry I'm ba - aack," he says in a singsong voice.

Bri yells at Robby, "Let her go, you don't wanna squish Seth's girl-friend on our first day at camp."

I look at Seth, wondering if everybody knows. He smiles back. I guess so.

"Nah," Robby says as he lets go, "I've got a better plan."

Robby starts wringing his hands together, "I saw at least three fat long snakes with Megan's name on 'em." Robby must remember my prank from last year. It's coming back to haunt me. I roll my eyes. I'm not afraid of snakes, but still, I don't want to find one in my bed.

Ashley and Kayla squeal, "Don't bring them in here!" "I won't be able to sleep." They keep chattering and squealing at the same time.

Bri answers, "Don't worry, I'm faster and better at catching snakes than Robby is, I'll put two in his bunk for every one he puts in ours."

Ashley and Kayla squeal again.

Seth turns to me and says, "I'll see you at dinner, I better get my stuff unpacked and chase down my cabin crew. I'm the first cabin on the right side," he reaches out and gives my hand one last squeeze.

I look at him anticipating when we can go to our 'secret place', hope-fully later tonight. "Okay, I'll see you then. Bye."

"Bye, snake haven!" Robby calls out as he follows Seth out the door.

The girls answer with one last squeal.

My cabin mates get down to the business of unpacking and jostling for position to each grab a drawer in the solitary dresser. The door creaks open and in walks Tasha, Tynekwa and Allison. I can tell by the looks on their faces that they are best buds now.

I get out my packet and sit at the desk to find out if the rules for naming our cabin are the same as last year. "Okay gang, we have to name our team something from nature except no animals." Last year it was animals.

Names start flying around the room in a huge free for all: Glaciers, snowballs, stars, rainbows, avalanche, tornados, hurricane, sunspots, volcanoes, Venus flytraps, seaweed, waterfalls, roses, daisies, eclipses, sunbeams, spider webs.

It turns out our team has a wicked sense of humor. After a lively debate, everyone votes for Ashley's suggestion, the 'Venus Flytraps'.

Tasha says, "I hope nobody else picks that name."

"Oh, I wouldn't worry about that. It's pretty original," I say.

Two raps on the cabin door and Mr. Z. (still glowing) sticks his head in the cabin door. "Hey girls, I've volunteered your cabin to hand out the hot dogs, chips and sodas for dinner tonight. Why don't you head on down and find Toby. Megan and I will meet you later."

The 'Venus Flytraps' head out laughing and chattering down the path.

"Megan let's go for a walk."

I follow Mr. Z. down the path to a couple of chairs set out on the boat landing. We have privacy while still being in view of the whole camp. We sit.

# Chapter Two

## Zadok

"Megan, when you look at me, what do you see?"

"You glow." I can't look at him as I say this; it sounds so strange.

"Do you see anyone else who a—'glows'?"

I look out at the lake, everything is so beautiful, "No."

I voice the only explanation I can think of that isn't supernatural, "Mr. Z. is there something wrong with you? Are you dying?"

Tears are welling up in my eyes. I take a deep breath and will myself not to get emotional. That must be the reason. Nothing else makes sense.

He chuckles, "No. But let me ask the questions. You'll get your chance in a minute. When did you first notice?"

"Last year."

"Have you told anyone, discussed this with anyone?"

"No. Except last year, when we were around the campfire, I mentioned you look like an angel. The kids teased me, so I never mentioned it again."

"Am I shining now?"

I look up at him, "Yes."

Now I'm getting scared. I'm afraid of what Mr. Z. is going to say next. I sense my world is changing, the same way water becomes an ice cube. It's still H2O, in a different form.

"Well you're right; you're not imagining things. Some people I can't hide from. Those that have the gift.[1] Like you." He looks me in the eye.

"Megan, what do you think I am?"

I can't breathe. This is the moment where I expand.

I whisper, "An Angel."

"My name is Zadok."

Suddenly his brightness arises.

I see wings. I see his glory. He is beautiful. He is air. He is real. I am small and earthy next to this immortal angel. Zadok cloaks himself once again in his human form. Unbelievably, no one else in camp seems to have noticed.

I am changed. I am forever. I am more. I am afraid.

*  *  *

"Megan, I am a messenger of God. I'm here to do what he wants.[2] You have the gift of seeing spiritual beings[3], that's why you can see me. If you can see me, you will also be able to see others. The good, and the bad."

"Others? The bad?" I'm still in shock. I can't think.

"It's in the Bible, Megan. We're in there. We are at war with the forces of darkness, even on a beautiful day like today."[4]

"When the evil ones notice you, and they will, you and your loved ones are going to be targets.[5] You need to be prepared.[6] They will come after you. You are in danger."

"You have eight days to ask me questions; you have the gift to see and the responsibility of free will.[7] You can choose to fight evil or join the devil and his angels."[8]

"But what can I do? How can I fight spiritual beings?"

I start to panic. Waves of fear slip over my head. I'm drowning in it.

"You can't, but He can," Zadok points to heaven. "God is in control and he's already won."[9]

I start to calm down as I realize Zadok is right. "Be still and know that I am God,"[10] I pull up from memory.

"That's right," Zadok smiles. "Every one on God's side has special gifts. Seeing angels, demons and other spiritual beings reminds you that we are involved in something much bigger than your universe, more mysterious, wonderful and dangerous than most people care to think about."

I let my fear go and keep repeating my simple scripture until I am calm.

I manage to smile at Zadok, pushing back my fear, "I can do this. I guess I have to."

"You were chosen for a reason," Zadok says. He gets up and stretches.

"Zadok," it feels funny calling him that, "why do you think God chose me?"

He looks at me and smiles, "I don't know for sure, but in the Bible, He indicates that a child's faith is powerful.[11] You are at the end of childhood. I remember when David, just a boy, slew a giant that a whole army of armed men were afraid to face.[12] Maybe you have that kind of faith." Zadok looks at me and smiles, but in his eyes I see that he is serious.

"Well Megan, talk to Him, tonight. You know He loves to hear from you. Now I have to go start a fire for the weenie roast. I'm still not sure if I'm brave enough to eat one of those things. We'll talk again soon," Zadok squeezes my shoulder then walks back up the path, still glowing.

I look out at the lake again. How do I act as if nothing has happened? Who can I tell? Who would believe me? No one. The wind in the trees behind me rustles the leaves; a cloud covers the sun and suddenly I feel chilled and threatened. Darkness begins to fall. The universe contracts and evil takes a step closer.

* * *

I look at all the kids running over to watch Mr. Z.; I mean Zadok, start the fire. With the extra flames behind him, I see his wings again outlined in the light. I guess it's true that nothing can be hidden in the light.[13]

I hear footsteps approaching on the dock, and see Seth and Robby, followed by Kayla and a girl I don't know.

"Come on Meg, let's help the kids," Seth says.

Robby pipes up, "Hey genius, tell her what you signed her up for tonight. He volunteered all of us for KP after dinner and making sure the fire goes out."

"Well, better tonight when there aren't any dishes to do and we get to stay up past curfew, till' the fire goes out," Seth answers.

"Oh, yeah. Good thinking," Robby turns to the girls, "Did you find enough sticks?"

He's talking about sticks to roast marshmallows after it gets dark. Kayla and the other girl look at Robby adoringly, while Kayla answers, "We're working on it. Don't worry; you can pick yours out first so you can show us how to do it." The girls head back toward the tree line.

Seth holds out a cup of coffee for me, "Here, I thought you might like one." He's drinking a coke. Robby takes a last swig of his Mountain Dew and crumples the can with one hand. I say, "You really should have saved that move for your fan club over there, nodding to Kayla and her friend."

"Oh, yeah, I'm the man, check out the guns," Robby says as he flexes his biceps.

I turn to Seth and say, "I've never really gotten what that means; someday you'll have to explain it to me." I take a sip and say, "Thanks for the coffee."

We start heading back to the campfire. Robby puts his can on the ground kicks it and yells, "Kick the can!" Several young hyper sugar fueled boys converge as Robby yells out directions and gets the game going.

Seth looks at me and shakes his head, "He never runs on anything less than full steam. I'm glad he's here. If he can't wear these kids out, no one can."

Now that we are at the campfire I say hi to some of the kids and staff, I haven't seen since last year. I can't believe how normal everything appears. I want to scream that there is a whole hidden world around us. There is no one who can see, no one to really believe. I work hard on getting anchored back into my every day life.

Mr. Steve along with Mr. Timmons, one of the owners, calls Seth over to help him roast the hot dogs. Mr. Timmons loads up these big metal tongs that hold a dozen dogs each. They're heavy, but the dogs can't fall out of them in to the fire.

I walk over to my Venus Flytrap girls who are standing behind the table loaded with buns, plates, and all the fixings' needed for a cook out. "Hey Megan, have some chips!" Five bags fly at me, hitting me mainly in the head. Somebody says, "A chip off the old block!"

Now they're all laughing so hard I'd almost bet someone's going to pee in their pants. Next someone yells out, "How 'bout a soda?" An empty can hits me on the shoulder. As I half duck, I spill some of my coffee. The laughter continues. I'm becoming more anchored by the minute.

Seth yells out, "I warned you you'd be in for it!"

The laughter goes on. I have an intuition that I'm definitely going to be finding at least a frog in my desk drawer tonight.

*   *   *

As the sun sets, I have the 3 musketeers as I'm beginning to think of them, Tasha, Allison and Tynekwa run back to get us all jackets and a couple of flash lights. I have a few minutes to think about how ordinary the night appears, except for the fact that I can see angels. I'm still in shock.

Mr. and Mrs. Davis are the leaders for the songs tonight. They're the adult team from Robby's bus. Mr. Davis comes out lugging a big box of bandanas. "Okay, who has names picked out for their cabins?" As each team yells out their name, followed by much hooting and hollering, Mr. Davis hands over a bag filled with their team's color. We get neon Orange. Seth's team, the 'Lightening Bolts' draws a bright blue color. Robby points out, "Hey put your colors together, go UF!" Robby is talking about the University of Florida, back home. He starts doing the gator chomp, along with the "Duh, da, duh, da, dudadudaduda." Robby's fan club squeals as he comes close.

Robby's team name is the "Volcanoes." They get bright red.

We settle back in to a light routine of singing songs and roasting/burning marshmallows. We end with a group prayer and Mr. Davis sends all the campers back to their cabins for bed. "Bri," I ask, "can you take charge till I get in?"

"Yep," she says as she takes a flashlight to lead our girls back.

Mr. Timmons comes up to Robby, Seth and I and says, "You kids know to dump some water on the fire once it dies down; watch out for the steam. Buckets are over by the shed, you can use the lake water. I'll be in the lodge kitchen making notes for the early breakfast gang. I'll be back out after that. See you in the morning."

We nod our heads and say, "Thanks Mr. Timmons."

After Mr. Timmons is out of sight, Robby turns to us and says, "I know I'm a fifth wheel."

I pipe up, "you mean a third wheel."

"Yeah, whatever, I've got my pole, I'm gonna head over to the dock to see if I can catch something."

Seth looks at him and says, "Thanks man."

Seth and I sit down next to each other with our backs to the dock facing out to the water now on our left. We can still see the cabins off to the right and the lodge behind them. Seth reaches out and grabs my hand. "I missed you," he says.

I squeeze his hand lightly, "I missed you too."

"You know I never officially asked you to be my girlfriend, but I am now."

Seth takes my other hand and stares lovingly into my eyes, "Would you?"

I smile at him and answer, "Yes, of course."

We lean in and give each other a kiss. His lips are warm. Seth smells smoky from the fire. I love that smell. He puts his hand on the back of my hair and holds me gently while we press our lips softly, searching, not wanting the moment to be broken. I breathe him in, wanting to hold this moment for eternity. We slowly draw away.

"There, sealed with a kiss. You don't mind if people know, do you?" Seth asks.

"I think they already know, from the way the girls were acting earlier."

"Well back home, I was texting you a lot, I think they noticed; and Robby's' probably said a few things to Bri and of course she tells everybody everything."

"Yeah, it's pretty hard to keep secrets."

The mention of secrets reminds me again about Mr. Z. /Zadok. For a moment, I had almost forgotten. I wonder if he sleeps while he's in human form. I wonder if he's watching us now from a different dimension, in spirit form. Suddenly, I have a million questions.

Seth asks, "What are you thinking?" I scoot closer and lean against him. I want to tell him my secret. I won't. Not yet. Instead, I think about us, our future.

"I'm just glad we have these eight days together," I say. Eight days with Seth, now my boyfriend, eight days to ask Zadok questions.

"Really only seven, today's almost over with," Seth says into my hair.

Seth continues, "I peeked at your schedule and traded with Carrie so I can do lifeguard duty this week with you."

"So you can see me in a swim suit?" I tease. Most of us girls wear t-shirts over our suits and only one pieces are permitted anyway.

"Nah. I don't care about that. I just want to spend as much time with you as I can."

"I'm glad, me too," Seth keeps his arm around my shoulder. I don't know what about him is so intoxicating. When I'm near Seth, it's just so right. Almost like we're one.

The fire makes a crackling sound as a log falls with a thump into the embers. I can feel the chill from the evening creeping closer. I shiver. The fire is dying and our time together is running out.

Robby strolls back, "Nothing's biting tonight. Whew, it's getting cold." He stands as close to the fire as he can get without stepping into it. He holds his hands up to warm them.

Seth stands up pulling me up with him, "Let's get those buckets and get to work." We each dip our buckets in the lake trying not to get our feet wet.

We throw our water on the embers and the steam makes a loud hissing sound.

Robby lowers his voice and says, "Steam fires of hell."

I feel a fingernail trailing down the center of my back and jump.

It was just Seth. "Boy are you jumpy," he laughs, "I'll walk you back to your cabin." Seth puts his arm around my shoulder, and with a flashlight in the other, we make our way back to my cabin.

We can here the girls giggling as we approach, so we just say goodbye as I head in.

As I enter, the cabin gets quiet until I hear croaking coming from my desk drawer. The girls burst out laughing at their little joke. I lift out the toad and let him go out the door. "Remember, I can pay it forward."

"And," I add menacingly, "I'm not afraid to pick up a snake."

The laughter quiets down to a giggle and soon they're asleep from exhaustion. I get ready for bed quickly, patting down my cot just in case the toad wasn't the only surprise.

# Chapter Three

## Unexpected Dangers

I awake to the sound of a bugle accompanied by the groans of everyone in the cabin. "It's too early," "Just 15 more minutes," someone moans. I force myself out of my cot feeling the same way. I'm stiff and my muscles ache from spending the night in the cot. I know not to stall on taking a shower, as the hot water will run out by third or fourth kid. Besides, the hot water will wake me up and warm up my muscles.

"Okay, any one left in bed by the time I get back from the shower, is fair game to hit with your pillows, and if you don't take a shower this morning, make sure you do during the lunch or after-dinner break," I grab my tote that holds my toiletries; wrap myself in my robe and head out the door.

I take a quick shower, leave some extra conditioner in my hair because of swimming duty, head back, get dressed, and race over to the counselors lounge for a cup of coffee. I'm not hungry, but I force myself to eat a bagel with cream cheese. I'll need the energy later. I say hi to the other early birds while waiting for Seth to walk in.

"Hey Megan," Carrie says as she comes in, "What's your schedule like?" She asks.

"I have archery in the morning and swimming in the afternoon," Carrie sounds excited. She's very athletic and it shows.

"Mine's swim in the morning and arts and crafts in the afternoon," I'm not a fan of the sun, and not nearly as athletic as Carrie. So I'm pretty happy with my assignment. We compare notes on the kids in our cabin. A few minutes latter, Robby and Seth stroll in together.

Robby says, "So this is where all the beautiful girls hang out." Carrie punches Robby as he walks by. "Ow, super woman that hurts," Robby says, feigning pain.

"Where there's coffee, there's Megan," Seth comes behind me and rubs my shoulders. "Did you already eat? Want me to grab you something?" he offers.

"I already had a bagel thanks."

"Let me get you a refill," I hand Seth my mug and he walks to the breakfast bar.

Carrie gives me a look, "Well look at the love birds."

I just smile, "Robby's available."

Carrie gives me a dirty look, "I'm not interested in Robby, a long distance relationship or any relationship right now. We're young, what's the rush? Can't we all be friends without getting into mushy stuff? It's just not for me right now."

"You're right, we are kind of young, but it just happened. Who knows how long we'll last? Besides, we are long distance most of the time, so our relationship won't go beyond us texting and hanging out a couple of times a year. I do know how I feel about him, I love Seth and I don't want to be with anybody else."

Mr. Z. (Zadok), walks in, talking to Mr. Timmons, I look at him and my brain goes in to shock. I hope it doesn't show on my face. I hadn't remembered this morning what had happened yesterday. I just woke up happy that Seth liked me as much as I liked him.

Seth brings a plate loaded with doughnuts and sits down next to me. He sets my refill down, then his plate and takes his can of Coke, out from under his arm.

"What's wrong? Are you Okay, you look like you've just seen a ghost."

I think, "no just an Angel," but I say, "I'm okay, just too much coffee before I ate. I'll be okay."

Seth says a quick prayer, and starts wolfing down his doughnuts. I feel guilty because I forgot to say grace, so I silently ask for forgiveness and say a quick thanks.

I start thinking of some other questions I need to ask Zadok. Am I the only one at camp who knows what he is? Are there others like me that I can talk to? Can I talk to people about him, people who can't see him? My mind is racing.

"Megan, did you bring sunscreen I forgot mine," Seth says.

He pops the top on his soda and takes a big slurp.

"Yeah, I have plenty."

Carrie looks at Seth in wonderment and says, "How much sugar can one person inhale? Six doughnuts and a coke."

"I'm eating light today 'cause of swimming, don't want to be weighed down."

Carrie looks at me, "He's kidding right?"

I shrug my shoulders, not really sure.

Seth swivels around looking for Robby. He spies him talking to a cute blonde a couple tables behind us. Seth asks, "Who is Robby talking to?"

"I think her name is Paige," I vaguely remember her from last year. She had seemed kind of shy.

Mr. Z. walks up to our table and says, "Good morning Carrie, Megan, Seth," looking at Seth he asks, "Can you check and make sure your kids know where they're going after chapel? I'm going to borrow Megan and get the preservers out for swim today."

"Okay, see you soon," Seth gives my hand a quick squeeze under the table before he gets up.

Zadok and I head out the door together toward the boathouse. It's slightly chilly out and I wish I had a jacket.

"I thought you might have some questions, for me."

I nod my head yes, and think of where to start.

"Is there anybody else here at camp who knows who you are?"

"No. Not currently. I'm sent where ever God wants, whenever He wants."

"Is there anybody I can talk to if," Zadok looks at me, "when,"[14] Zadok nods his head with approval glad I had caught my slip up, "things start to happen with these bad angels?"

"Pray,"[15] Zadok answers.

"No," I say thinking he's misunderstanding me.

"I understand what you mean," Zadok says, "Just because you can see angels doesn't mean that you get any special way to deal with them. Just like when Jesus walked the earth and the devil came to visit him.[16] He didn't call on us to help: He came here to fulfill his role as a Holy sacrifice.

"You have the same defense he has. God's word. If you need saving, use his word, the Bible, if that doesn't work, leave it up to Him.[17] You can't fight an angel on your own anyway. Angels are stronger, faster, and smarter than you.[18] We move between the earthly realm and the spiritual.[19] You, however, are bound by the rules of earth. The devil and his demons are not. For now, you are trapped here; earth is in the hands of the prince of this world, the devil.[20] Remember the devil can harm you, but he can't kill you with out God's permission. Keep that in mind."

We reach the boathouse. Zadok pauses and looks out at the lake. Zadok looks serious, concerned. He continues, "If God allows the evil angels to hurt you, it is only to make you stronger."[21] We enter the boathouse.

"Look, if you tell other humans you can see angels, most of them are going to think you're a kook. Others will become so fascinated with the spiritual realm they will be distracted from their salvation.[22] There are very, very few who can handle the knowledge of spiritual forces and not be distracted from their Creator. You must be very selective of who you share this knowledge with."

I can't think. All my other questions have evaporated along with the morning chill. The sun is shining as Zadok loads up my arms with preservers. We carry them down to the beach. They smell slightly moldy. Nothing like the smell of mold to bring you back down to earth, I think.

"Don't worry, be happy,"[23] Zadok chuckles at his joke and I do too.

"You still haven't asked me the most important question, but that will come later."

"The most important thing? I can tell I have some serious thinking to do, besides my relationship with Seth."

The chapel bell begins to ring. "Are you going?" I ask.

"Of course. Even though it's only a shadow of Heaven[24], it's where I feel most at home, here on earth. Remember, I live to worship my Lord,"[25] We walk in silence to the chapel.

I'm still trying to absorb my new reality and what it means.

I do feel I am living in a shadow, that the meaning is obscured. I'm missing something. As we enter, Zadok repeats, "Don't worry, be happy."

I let the joy rise in my heart as the worship service starts.

\* \* \*

After chapel, Seth and I along with Mr. Z. and Jackson, one of the older teens I don't know that well, head down to the beach. Jackson gather's everyone one around and explains the rules for a swim and run race. Mr. Z. climbs up the lifeguard tower. Seth is assigned to watch the boys and I, the girls.

This should be a piece of cake.

\* \* \*

The water is chilly and takes my breath away; so I do what I've always done, take a deep breath and go under all the way. There is a swim platform only about twenty five feet out in the lake; the kids start to swim toward it.

Seth, a fast swimmer, is already up on the platform with most of the boys and one or two of the girls. I stay in the shallows watching and constantly counting bobbing heads. Jackson is further up on the beach tying flags on a string for the relay teams to rip off, as they come up on shore and race across the sand.

I hear a scream, "Let go!" one of the girls, who is more than half-way to the platform goes under. All I see is bubbles. Zadok and Seth yell simultaneously. Seth dives in, while I grab a preserver and start swimming to the last location of the bubbles. Time slows down, the drag from the preserver is worse than in practice. Seth has reached the bubbles and goes under looking for the little girl. I'm almost at the bubbles, just two or three feet away. I start to pray without consciously thinking, Oh God please let us find her, let her be okay, Seth surfaces, "I can't find her!" I hear panic in his voice. He takes three quick breaths and goes under again. I do the same. Jackson has reached us; I can vaguely hear his muffled voice as I go under. Opening my eyes, I swim for the bottom. The lake water is murky and long tendrils of seaweed caress and tug at my legs and arms. I look to my left and see a flash of pink. I also, see a horrible black image pulling at the girl trying to keep her down. She's screaming under water swallowing it, pushing the thing away. The girl is drowning before my eyes. My heart races at the sight. Suddenly Seth swims into view. He is pulling the little girl up and I follow them to the surface. I look down below us and see a dark shadowy hand reaching toward us. I start to panic hoping the preserver is nearby in case it tries to pull one of us under again. When my face breaks through the water, I see my preserver floating a few feet away. I grab it and Jackson pulls it over the little girls head. Seth and Jackson start for the platform; it's closer than the shore. The girl isn't conscious.

I look over my shoulder to the beach and see Zadok on the shore, and then he's gone. I look back to the platform and there he is. He helps pull the girl out and Seth and Jackson pull themselves up. I struggle up onto the platform by myself. Watching for any sign of the watery shadow.

Zadok rolls the girl on her side, then quickly on her tummy, to get as much water out as possible. "Get the boat," he says to Jackson. He rolls her onto her back, and then checks her mouth for obstructions. We start CPR. He breathes into her mouth while I do chest compressions. Almost immediately, she starts to cough up water and breathe.

She starts to cry, gagging and coughing up the last of the fluid in her lungs.

"It's okay, sweetie, you're okay, we're getting the boat," I say.

I look at her legs. They are covered with scratch marks. What ever was pulling at her, it was real. I shudder.

The other kids start talking. Seth takes charge of them. Jackson pulls up in the boat as I talk to her and try to calm her down.

Zadok picks up the girl and steps into the boat to take her to shore. I hear her say, "Somebody kept pulling me under. He was trying to kill me. Don't make me get in the water."

As they pull away, all the talk on the platform is about the near drowning. No one mentions seeing a dark presence in the water; and I guess I'm the only one to notice Mr. Z.'s sudden appearance on the platform and the fact that except for where Mr. Z. touched the girl, his clothes are dry. Most of the kids swim to shore. I'm too afraid to get in the water. The kids assume I'm too tired after the rescue. I keep looking at the lake. I think I see a dark shadow hanging out near the far shore. I wait for someone to bring the boat to get me. When I get back to shore, I'm spooked. An unseen danger is watching and hunting.

*   *   *

Later that evening, after dinner, I'm excused from KP duty, because of what happened during swim. I go to the bathroom and head for a stall. As I'm locking the door, I hear someone else run in and go to a stall, two down from mine. I hear a gag and then puking. I ask, "Are you okay?" Whoever it is, doesn't answer and then I hear footsteps leaving. Strange.

I find Seth at his cabin and we walk to 'our place'. He holds out his hand for me to step down onto the dock and we sit. Seth puts his arm around my shoulder and I rest my head on his.

"I'm so glad that girl's okay," he says.

"You saved her life," I hug him.

"Wow, you think, 'what would I do if something like that happens' but you never really think its going to happen, ya know?"

"Yeah, you're a hero and you're my hero," I say.

"I'm going to write my parents and tell them what happened. I've never written them a letter from camp before. They'll probably pass out from shock," Seth laughs.

I wonder if I should tell him about the dark presence pulling the girl under. If I do, will he believe me? I decide not to risk it. I change the subject.

"Are you going to tell them about us?"

"I don't have to Meg, they read all my texts; they know we like each other. My Dad did talk to me about treating you right and I will 'cause you're my girl now."

Pebbles start hitting us in the head, on the dock and the water. We look up and there's Robby, "Had to stop it before you two start getting too romantic. Oh Seth, Oh Megan." Robby adds some kissing noises for extra effect.

I laugh and find some stray pebbles on the dock to start pelting him.

Seth jumps up and goes to tackle Robby. "Look man, we've only got six more days and then it's back to long distance. Let me have some time with my girl."

"Hey, don't get mad at me, Mr. Z. sent me down to get you guys for the camp fire. He told me where to find you."

"Have you guys noticed anything different about Mr. Z?" I ask as we start to walk back to the camp. Seth takes my hand.

"No. Except that he's onto you two," Robby says.

Seth says, "No, why?"

"Nothing. You're right. He's just keeping a closer eye on us," I can't tell Robby or Seth what I know.

I was hoping they had seen Zadok today disappearing from the beach, and reappearing on the dock, his dry clothes, and the dark presence in the water or the mysterious scratch marks on the girl's legs. But nobody noticed, except me.

*   *   *

I was looking forward to having more time alone with Seth tonight, but I don't think Zadok is going to let that happen. I'm not sure if that's the human role he's playing or if it's from a spiritual order. I should be trying to figure out the question I'm supposed to ask, but all I really want right now is more time with Seth. Is that so wrong? I know it's not. It's normal. I can't be expected to be more than what I am. I don't want to deal with other realm things. I just want to be in the here and now.

I'm a teenager, what can I possibly do to help God and his angels? Why don't they just do what needs to be done? I wrack my brain for an answer.

What can I possibly do to help . . . Now I feel like an idiot. That must be the question. Okay, Zadok now I know what I need to ask. Then maybe you can leave Seth and me alone with what little time we have left.

I was right; Seth and I are not left alone for one minute at the campfire or after. Everyone wants to hear the story of how Casey (I found out her name) almost drowned.

*   *   *

The bugle wakes us up again. I have my question ready for Zadok when I can get him alone again. Its day three and only five more to spend with Seth. I gather my stuff and head for the showers, yawning along the way. Back at the counselors lounge, I run into Carrie again and we wait for the guys. Robby and Seth show up a few minutes later, and today Robby joins us for breakfast.

I notice Carrie seems to have taken more care with her appearance. I even see a hint of lip-gloss. She tosses her pigtails and asks, "Hey, Robby do you know where I can go to get more arrows for archery? The kids lost quite a few in the trees, and I'm not tall enough to reach them."

"I'll help you get them down," Robby says taking the bait, "I can show you where Mr. Timmons keeps the extra supplies too."

"Would, you? Thanks," Carrie says practically batting her eyelashes.

I just about fall off the bench in amazement. Carrie does so like Robby. I remember her climbing trees last year showing off her skill to everyone.

Nobody could climb higher than she could. Seth and I give each other a look, while Carrie and Robby discuss some of the finer points of archery. Robby's always so busy looking for the next joke that he doesn't always notice the obvious.

"Hi Robby," Paige the pretty girl Robby talked to at breakfast yesterday says.

"Oh, hi Paige," Robby says, he looks back to Carrie, and says, "Ah, Carrie, have you met Paige?"

"No. Hi. Would you like to sit with us?" Carrie's voice doesn't sound that friendly.

"Sure," Paige sits. Carrie and Robby keep talking trying to include Paige in the conversation; but they soon forget about her.

Seth and I talk about our cabin kids. We're just enjoying each other's company while we can before chapel starts. "Let's sit in chapel together, my kids on one side and yours on the other. They can't stop us from worshiping together," Seth says. I agree.

All the coffee I drank goes through me so I head over to the rest room before chapel starts.

While in the stall, I hear someone run in to the stall next to mine. I see pink sneaks, and then I hear a gag and retching. "Are you okay?" I ask.

I don't get an answer and the next thing I know, pink sneaks is running out of the bathroom. Deja-Vu.

I don't think 'pink sneaks' is sick. It's happened twice now, after meals. I'm thinking someone's bulimic. I remember watching a show on girls with eating disorders. One girl would go and throw up after a meal so she wouldn't gain any weight. I think 'pink sneaks' has the same problem, but first I have to find out who she is. It's time to play detective.

I head to chapel, Seth and my Venus girls have saved a place for me. My group is sitting near the back row. I look for 'pink sneaks' as I walk down the center aisle but I only see one girl wearing pink shoes and she looks too small. She must be sitting up near the front. I'll have to wait until after chapel to continue my search.

As we leave chapel, my Venus girls distract me. By the time I look for 'pink sneaks', most the kids are out the door. I catch a glimpse of a blonde girl with shoulder length hair wearing pink shoes, running towards the archery area. I catch Carrie on her way to the range and ask her, "Carrie there's a blonde girl in your next class who's wearing pink sneakers; they're really cute, can you ask her where she got them?"

"Sure, see you at lunch," she says.

I catch up to Seth walking to the beach.

"Hey, handsome, you can rescue me today."

"From what, a 'Venus flytrap?" Seth says. I lightly put my hand on his chest, stopping him.

"If I find a snake in my cabin, kind sir, will you come and get it out?" I say as I practice flirting with Seth.

"Yes, fair maiden, I will rescue you from the fierce legless dragon, slay him, skin him, and turn him into a fashionable belt as a reminder of the day your true love rescued you from the clutches of the slithery serpent."

Seth waves his imaginary sword, grabs me around the waist, and swings me around.

"Stop!" I laugh.

"You asked for it."

The kids on the beach start hooting and hollering for Seth as we make our way down to them.

Mr. Z is gathering all the kids down by the relay flags. Half of them are stripping down to their suits. Others are slathering sunscreen on, horsing around, awaiting instructions. Mr. Z. grabs everyone's attention by saying, "Update on Casey, she's fine, they're keeping her at the hospital over night for observation. Good job Seth, Megan, and Jackson. You really pulled together as a team and that saved that little girl's life. I'm proud of you. Now let's have a race."

After swim, we head up to lunch. Seth and I grab some sandwiches and sodas, it's too nice of a day to eat indoors. I quickly scan the room, looking for Carrie, but she's nowhere in sight.

"Want to go down to our place and eat?" Seth asks.

"Great idea, I'd love to," we head out with our lunch. The day is beautiful. A light breeze keeps blowing hair into my face. I wish I'd brought a hair tie. I want to tell Seth about Zadok, but I'm afraid he'll think there's something wrong with me. How do you tell your boyfriend that one of your camp counselors is an angel? Especially since Seth's never noticed anything out of the ordinary about him. How would I bring up that I see Mr. Z. glowing? How do I tell him about the evil things I'm seeing too?

What if Seth stops treating me normal and all he wants to do is talk about what I see or worse yet, if he doesn't want to be with me anymore because I'm too strange? Or what if he doesn't believe me?

I can't risk it. I just have to hope he notices something, and then I can bring up what I know.

There is a safer topic I can discuss. We sit on the dock and watch an eagle circling, hunting for fish on the far end of the lake. We eat our sandwiches, sitting so close our legs are touching. I throw one of my legs over his, swinging them together just over the water. I ball up some bread and throw it in the lake. Perch and Sunfish rise up to the surface to eat it.

"I think one of the girls here is bulimic."

"Great topic for lunch," Seth says.

"Oh, yeah, I guess it is kind of gross."

"So who is it?"

"I don't know yet. I only saw her shoes. They were pink."

"Well that certainly narrows it down."

"If I find out who it is, what should I say to her?"

"Hm, what does one say to a cookie tosser? What's up?" "Lunch."

I hit Seth, "Stop. It's not funny."

"I guess you should probably tell one of the adults and let them handle it. Megs, whoever the cookie tosser is, she's going to need help. Professional help. You aren't going to solve her problems in the next five days."

"Well I can try to talk to her, if I can find out who she is."

Seth stands and holds out his hand, to help me up. I don't let go once I'm up. I know Zadok is out there watching me. Having a guardian angel, at moments like this, is a little irritating. I look up at Seth; he's looking down at me. He wants to kiss me and I long to kiss him. Seth lowers his head to mine. I lift my face to him. Seth puts his hands on my hips and draws me closer. I lay my hands gently on his chest. Our lips touch as a flash of darkness in the trees catches my eye. We both hear a branch snap and look back into the woods. Seth and I see a deer and its fawn bounding out of sight, deeper into the woods. I shiver. Seth puts his hands on my arms and rubs them, our romantic tension broken.

"It's okay, it's only a deer," Seth says. Except it's not okay, because just past where the deer were, I see something evil, watching us, watching me. I know Seth can't see it, but I get an uneasy feeling; it knows I can.

"Let's go back; I have to do a couple of things back at the cabin," I say. I avoid looking back into the woods where the evil thing is hiding. I grab Seth's' hand, "Can you walk me back?" I try to sound playful, not scared. I silently ask God to protect us; it's too soon, I'm not ready to deal with my gift yet. Just a few minutes ago, I desperately didn't want Zadok around and now I pray he is.

When I get back to the cabin, all the girls are in. I feel better having them around. Tynekwa, Tasha and Allison, my three musketeers, are in my arts and crafts class. Today, we'll be making wallets, purses or belts out of leather piece kits. They're discussing what they like best. I avoid looking out the windows, afraid of what I might see. I'm glad to have the girls walk me to the crafts room.

Class goes by fast. Afterwards, I head over to help cook dinner. Mr. Steve is in charge of dinners. Tonight is spaghetti night; I'm put to work boiling the noodles. The kitchen quickly gets hot. With sauce, frying meat, and garlic bread going, the temperature soon rises to an uncomfortable level. I'm glad we'll be having another weenie roast tomorrow night. As I stir and sweat, I look around quickly at the other kids feet, but 'pink sneaks' isn't here.

Thankfully, we set everything out in less than half an hour. As the dinner bell rings, I go outside the kitchen door, craving the breezy fresh air. I'm careful not to look at the woods, but I am actively looking for Seth. The air outside is cool compared to the heat of the kitchen. Out front, I spy Carrie with some of the kids from her cabin, I run over to join her; I'm still spooked from what I saw in the woods. It must be a dark angel in some form. I plan to talk to Zadok about what I saw as soon as dinner is over. I know it can't hurt me with out God's permission, but seeing something like that is just plain freaky.

"Carrie," I ask, "did you find out who, I mean where she got the shoes?"

Carrie gives me a funny look. "Why didn't you just ask her yourself?"

"What do you mean?" I say.

"This morning, at breakfast. Paige was sitting right with us. Any way, she got them last year, she doesn't remember where."

Paige is 'pink sneaks'? I'm shocked. Somehow, I didn't think it would a counselor. I'll have to get her alone and ask her.

"Oh, well thanks for asking," I change the subject. "So, how did arrow hunting go?" I ask trying to keep a smirk off my face.

"Fine," Carrie smiles, "Robby is really nice when he's not joking around. I think Paige likes him and there's always a group of the younger girls following him around."

"I call the younger girls his fan club. He is cute and always willing to play; no wonder they all have a crush on him."

"He's a good friend to have," Carrie says, "I'm enjoying hanging out with him."

"Have you seen Robby and Seth?" I ask.

"I think Mr. Timmons has them taking the canoes out of the boat house and cleaning them for our trip to the dam tomorrow." Carrie says.

"Oh, is that tomorrow?" I'd forgotten.

You have to be strong enough to paddle to the dam and back. Each canoe only holds three campers. All the canoes are florescent orange so every one on the water knows we're from camp. Also, the bright orange canoes, make it easier to find someone if they get lost or lag behind. On the trip we stop for lunch at the dam, rest a little bit, then head back. All the campers are required to wear a life vest in case of tipping. Counselors get to sit on floating cushions, in case they have to swim to help a camper. Everyone tips on purpose or by accident. Either way, you're going over and out at least once. It's a lot of fun.

The only bad thing you have to watch out for is the king snakes. They're not poisonous, but they are surprising. The king snakes like to hang over the water from tree branches. Usually, at least once a summer, someone gets a snake in their canoe. The trick is to stay away from the trees. But the newbies don't know that.

I decide to head down to the boathouse; maybe I can help.

Sure enough Robby, Seth, and Mr. Timmons along with Mr. Davis are carrying the last of the canoes down to the beach. I head up to the boathouse to carry the rest of the life preservers down. The dust in the boathouse makes me sneeze. I hear some scuttling in a nearby corner, behind a pile of canvass covers. I look up as a cheeky little chipmunk gives me a warning chirp.

I answer, "Thanks I'll be careful." He gives me a couple more chirps then heads under some boards. Seth walks in just as I sneeze again.

"God bless you," he says.

"I love it when you catch me doing something graceful like sneezing my head off."

Seth comes up and helps load my arms up with preservers, "You're cute no matter what you do." he puts his hands on my shoulders and lightly touches his nose to mine; he gazes into my eyes, we smile. He lets go and then carries the remaining preservers out.

When we walk down to the beach, Mr. Davis is hosing out the insides of the canoes to remove the spider webs.

"You kids can go up to dinner, we'll finish up," he says. Robby comes trotting up to us, waves and continues past us. Seth and I slowly walk up to the mess hall, enjoying our few minutes of private time.

"I think I found out who the bulimic is."

"Do you want to tell me?"

"Not yet, 'cause I'm not sure. I'm going to talk to her. If she's the one, maybe I can convince her to get help. If she won't, I can be a friend until she is ready. If she is the one, I'll have to convince her to tell an adult. She'll probably hate me, and won't want to be friends anyway."

Seth reaches out and takes my hand, "Sometimes it's hard to do the right thing, but it's always worse to do nothing."

"You're right. Thanks for listening."

"Well, it's easier to listen to you than to Robby burping the alphabet."

"At least I know where I stand," I punch him on the arm.

We reach the hall and go in to eat. After we sit, I look around for Paige. Luckily, she's sitting at a table with Robby, Carrie, and his growing fan club. I decide to follow her after dinner. As Paige gets up to leave, I ask, "Seth can you clear my tray? I'll meet up with you later."

"Sure, I'll see you at the campfire."

I head out after Paige trying not to be too obvious that I'm following her. She ducks in the bathroom and I hear retching as soon as I open the door. Paige comes out of the stall and sees me at the door.

"I think we better talk," I say.

"I just wasn't feeling well, I'm better now," Paige says.

"I know that's not true; I've heard you the past few days. I think you have a problem. We need to talk."

"Really? It's none of your business," Paige pushes past me out the door.

"Paige, please, just for a few minutes."

Paige stops and turns around to face me, "Look, I'm just dieting to lose a few pounds. I'm going to stop soon, so it really is none of your business. Why don't you go find a way to sneak around some more with your boyfriend and leave me alone." With that, she runs off in the direction of her cabin.

"Well that went well," I say under my breath.

Now what do I do? I need to try and talk to Paige again. I decide to attempt to talk to her one more time tomorrow. If that doesn't work, I'll need a new game plan.

Next, I go back to the mess hall, and peak in looking for Zadok. He's not there. I search the rest of the building, no luck. I run into Kayla and Bri and head back to our cabin with them. I glance casually at the woods and see the dark presence again. My heart sinks to my stomach; it is watching me. Please God, send Zadok back my way soon. I really don't want to deal with this on my own. I hope he's going on the canoe trip with us tomorrow. I can't stand the thought that the dark thing might be in the woods the whole way down the river. At the cabin, I grab a jacket, a flashlight and ask, "Can you girls wait for me?" Bri jokes, "Sounds like your afraid."

"Yep that's me, afraid of the dark," I say. They think I'm kidding.

As Bri and Kayla wait for me, I leave a light on in the cabin. We always return from campfire in the dark with our flashlights. I know its silly, but it does make me feel safer, having a beacon of light to come home to.

Zadok is with a group of young boys on the dock fishing. I excuse myself from Kayla and Bri and run over to him.

"Did ya catch anything?" I say as I walk out on the dock.

"We've caught 3 Sunfish and one Perch!" One of the boys says excitedly.

He opens a bucket to show me his catch.

I look at him and smile, "Wow, you're doing great."

I turn to Mr. Z. and ask, "Can I speak to you alone, for a few minutes?"

Mr. Z. says, "Sure, let me get one of the Jr. Staff here to help the kids."

I see Jada, one of the Jr. Staff like me, down on the beach. I'm about to call out when Mr. Z. says, as if reading my thoughts (which I know he can't do), "Some one who's not afraid to bait a hook or take a fish off the line."

"Oh," I say.

That narrows the list of prospects down. I see Toby coming down to the beach from the boy's cabin area. I wait until he's with in shouting distance and call him over. Zadok hands his pole over to Toby and we walk over to stand in front of the boathouse.

Knowing we could be interrupted at any time I blurt out, "I know what the question I need to ask is, but now I'm seeing a dark presence. It's mainly staying in the woods. I think it knows I can see it. What can I do about it.? I'm scared."

"Okay, first things first. Of course you can see, 'it'. You know you can see spiritual forces. But what you're forgetting is that they've always been there, even when you couldn't see them. Remember the devil, his angels, and demons walk about the earth, looking for those who are spiritually weak.[26] They want to steal their beginning faith from them.[27]

A camp like this is one of the best places for that, since many kids make their first profession of faith here."

"Yeah, but this is freaking me out," I say.

"Well you're going to have to learn to live with it," Zadok says matter of factly.

"So what's the question?" Zadok asks.

"How can I use my 'gift', wait I can say this better, what does God want me to do with my special talent?"

"Congratulations, Megan you asked the right question. Now find the answer," Zadok answers. He walks back to the campfire signaling my time today with him is done.

I groan. This is too hard. Why can't Zadok just tell me? I didn't even get to ask if he's here to protect me like a guardian angel kind of thing; but if he is, wouldn't I have more than eight days to ask him questions? I'm down to five days now and at this rate, I'm not going to learn the things I need to know before I leave camp.

What's going to happen when I'm in a more populated place? Am I gonna see these evil things everywhere? I remember from science class that germs are everywhere, but we can't see them. I'm grateful I can't see them. I'll just pretend they're like germs. But what happens when one speaks to me? I know God's totally in charge, but I'm still just trying to deal with my new scary reality.

Seth and Robby are walking down to the campfire with a bunch of kids. I'm not going to worry about it anymore tonight. I'm just going to enjoy being with Seth. I'll have more time to think about everything on the canoe trip tomorrow.

Seth and I manage to have a nice evening with the kids at the campfire. He picks me up and even gives me a piggyback ride.

We take any chance to touch that can't be deemed 'off limits' because it's too romantic. Afterwards, he walks the girls and me back to our cabin.

I don't see the dark presence; I'm not sure if that's because it's dark out or because it's gone for now. We say goodbye, excited about the canoe trip tomorrow.

After lights out, I keep waking with each little noise. I pray for God to protect me as I sleep, I know he will, but each new noise makes my mind race. The last time I look at my watch by the light of the moon, it's after 3 o'clock. Soon after, I fall into a disturbing sleep filled with dreams of large snakes chasing me. In my dream, I feel a hand resting on my stomach; I wake up and realize the feeling is still there. I roll over and the hand moves to my side. Now I'm terrified, I try to scream and nothing comes out. I feel the hand move up my side towards my head . . . The hand pushes my face firmly into my pillow, suffocating me. I find the courage and strength to scream.

Suddenly, the presence is gone. At the same time, my girls wake up. "Hey, what's going on? Is everyone okay?"

I reach for my flashlight and turn it on. I say, "It's okay, someone had a bad dream." I'm too embarrassed to tell them I'm the one who screamed.

I look at the clock, it's just before four. I lay back down gripping my flashlight. I don't know how I can possibly sleep tonight or any night for the rest of my life. I wish I didn't know those things are out there, or in here. I close my eyes and pray, it's the only thing I can do.

*   *   *

At the morning wake up call, my head is pounding. I take some ibuprofen and head over to the mess hall for some coffee. I hunt down a thermos to take on the trip, so I can have a steady infusion of caffeine. I help Mrs. Timmons finish packing sandwiches, chips and sodas in the coolers. Mr. Timmons and Jackson carry them down to the canoes. I have sunscreen, mosquito spray, ibuprofen and the thermos in my duffle. I'll tie it to one of the rails in the canoe so I don't lose it when, not if, the canoe tips over. I'm wearing my visor and sunglasses along with my swimsuit under my oversized T-shirt and shorts. Nothing fancy 'cause I know I'm getting wet.

On the beach, about fifty kids and ten counselors are busy breaking into groups of three to load up the canoes. Seth has volunteered us to take the coolers, which means no third person in our canoe. Robby and Carrie are traveling along with Paige in another. Well, that should be interesting.

Mr. Timmons sits everyone down to listen to the rules. "Float vests on all the kids. Camp counselors have float cushions. Tie anything to the inside of the canoe you don't want to lose; put toilet paper in a waterproof Ziploc bag. Potty breaks are in the woods. Use leaves if your canoe doesn't have any dry TP. Make sure the leaf you use isn't poison ivy, if you're not sure, ask someone." Lots of snickering follows these comments.

"There is a first aid kit in every canoe. Lunch is when we get to the dam. Put on your sunscreen now. Bring a hat and sunglasses if you have them. If you get lost, stay with your canoe; we will find you. If a stranger offers to help, ask them to contact the camp and give us your location. Mr. Davis and Toby are in the lead canoe, along with Angela (one of our new campers); Jackson and I will bring up the rear. We leave in 5 minutes. Have Fun."

Seth and I get in our canoe and push off the shoreline. We wait about fifty feet off the shore. The kids who haven't canoed before do quite a bit of zigzagging. We wait until some of the campers pass us and take our place in the middle of the pack.

After a while, we have enough distance that we can speak privately without being overheard.

"Did you get a chance to confirm who miss bulimia is?" Seth asks.

"Yeah. She doesn't think she has a problem. I'm going to ask her to get help one more time, if she won't, I guess I'll have to ask Mrs. Timmons for advice."

"Who is it?" Seth asks. I know he won't tell any one, but I'm uncomfortable telling him. If I don't tell him, he might get mad at me.

"Come on you can trust me," Seth says.

"I know," I say, "It's Paige."

"Wow, really? She's pretty, why would she do something like that?"

"I don't know. She doesn't want to talk about it," At least not to me.

"Please don't act any differently around her, okay?" I'm totally feeling guilty now that I told Seth.

"I don't talk to her or anything. I've kind of been distracted by this other hot chick," he says grinning at me. "If I can only get her alone, without two coolers separating us."

"Everywhere we go at camp, I feel like we're being watched," I think of Zadok.

"Well we are," Seth says, "everyone knows about us, so they're never going to let us be alone. At least not for a few years, until we're old enough to be engaged."

"Do you think we'll last that long?" I ask.

"Why not? I have an Aunt and Uncle that met in high school, and they're still married. Age doesn't have anything to do with how I feel about you Megs, I love you."

I turn around in the canoe; I can't see anyone ahead or behind us. I climb over one of the coolers; Seth leans over to meet me. I give him a kiss, and say, "I love you too." As I pull back and stand up the canoe wobbles. I lose my balance and fall in the water. I hear Seth laughing as my head breaks through the water.

He leans over and helps pull me back in; I'm tempted to pull him in, but I don't. "You look beautiful even when you're half drowned."

"I should 'a known I'd fall in. I've never made it one trip dry."

We keep paddling and talking as the sun dries me off.

When we get to the dam, Seth and I go for a swim. Mr. Davis and Toby eat with the kids on the shore. Seth and I swim across to the other side where there are some big boulders that we can sit on in plain view of every one else. For now, we stay in the water where we can hold hands under the surface or I can rest my legs on his, without being seen.

"I wish we lived closer to each other," I say.

"Well my parents said they'd take us (meaning Seth and his little brother Sammy) to Busch Gardens this summer. They said we could swing by and pick you up, if you pay your way."

"That would be great. Of course I'll come."

"We can always plan to go to college together and maybe next summer when we're sixteen, we can volunteer to one of those summer work programs then we'd have a whole month together."

Carrie and Robby swim over to join us. "Hey guys," Carrie says, "having fun?"

Robby comes up and pushes Seth's head under water. They start to play wrestle in the water so Carrie and I climb up on to the boulders to get out of the way.

"How's it going with you, Robby and Paige?" I ask.

"I like Robby and I think Robby likes me," Carrie says, "but Paige wants Robby pretty bad. The only reason she's not over here now is she's afraid to swim over. Robby's being nice to her, but I think he's made it clear that he would like to spend some time alone with me, but she's not taking the hint. I'm not sure what to do."

"Robby did ask Mr. Timmons to take Paige in their canoe on the way back. I don't think she's going to be happy about that. In a way, I don't see why Robby doesn't like her. She's prettier than me."

"Carrie, Robby's not that shallow. You are pretty, but you're also athletic and you get him. You're more his type. I can totally see why he'd rather be with you."

Carrie smiles at me, "Thanks, that makes me feel better." With that, Carrie stands up and cannonballs into the water. She swims over to Robby where they proceed to get into a splash fight.

Seth swims over to me, "Lets race back, loser has to," but I jump in and start to swim as hard as I can before he can finish his sentence.

On the way back, Seth tries to tip over the canoe more than once, but the coolers help keep it weighted. I think Robby's rubbed off on him.

*   *   *

I see the dark thing twice on our way back. Always lurking, watching, waiting. Halfway home, on the return trip, we stop at an inlet where there is a rope swing. Seth and I each take a turn. The water is only about five feet deep, not enough where people can dive in but deep enough to break your fall from the swing. The water is clear here, without weeds. I'm still rattled by the dark thing out there, but I don't want my fear showing. As Seth and I are going back to shore, for another turn on the swing, I stop paralyzed with fear. I grab for Seth. A sinister presence is attached to the swing as one of the boys, Charlie, gets ready to jump. I see it holding him in place as he tries to drop in the water. It doesn't let go until he's back over land. I hear a sickening crack as he lands on a rock. His arm is broken. You can see part of the bone pushing against the skin. Charlie starts to scream in pain.

Mr. Timmons comes rushing over yelling, "Bring the first aid kit."

Mr. Timmons lines the bone back up and puts on an inflatable cast.

Luckily, there's a cabin in sight. An older couple on the porch saw what happened. They come running up, "We can drive you to the hospital."

I look around for the presence but it's gone. I decide to treat it like a germ, I know it's there; and it's dangerous. For me, right now, that's the only way I can cope. In the back of my mind, a small voice tells me I'm not going to be able to ignore it for long and that I had better come up with a better strategy. My carefree days are numbered.

I try to catch Zadok that evening around the campfire, but our team activities keep me busy; all too soon, its lights out and I just have to wait for a new day.

Going to sleep is a challenge. I pray for protection and finally exhaustion wins. I fall into a deep dreamless sleep.

After the canoe trip, I don't want to give the dark presence an 'in' with any kids. I can't prevent accidents but maybe I can help curb self-destructive behavior.

Today I'm determined to talk to Paige. I have to convince her to get help. I think she already hates me for knowing her secret. One way or another, I'm going to have to be more persuasive.

Today also, starts the last three days I have with Seth. Just being near him makes me happy; I can't stand the thought that we have to go back to a long distance relationship. The worst part is knowing that we live only three and a half hours apart. Jacksonville isn't that far away from Clearwater. It may as well be across the country. Also, when school starts, what if he finds someone he likes better? I can't even think about that.

I shower and get to the mess hall as quick as I can. I miss Seth and want to see him as soon as possible. For once, he's beat me in. I meet him up by the food. We can't do anything except talk because of the adults in the room. We take our breakfast to the table and sit next to each other.

From where we're sitting, I can see into the main dining room whenever the door swings open. For a minute, I can't believe my eyes. The dark thing is in there. The door swings shut. Seth is talking to me, but I didn't hear what he said.

"Excuse me; I'll be back in a minute." I go through the door into the main dining room. The dark thing is hovering over by two boys I don't know. Zadok is nowhere in sight.

I know I must go over and let God use me to stop whatever is about to happen. I ask God to protect me, then I walk over to the boys and the dark angel. My hands are shaking, so I quickly fold my arms hoping no one else notices. I remember that this dark spiritual force is here to destroy or 'snatch' one of their faiths or to tempt them to do evil. I must do my best to stop it.

I come up and sit on the bench across from them waiting for something brilliant to pop into my mind. Something so powerful and obviously from God that this evil angel will turn and flee.

So of course, I say, "Hi."

I wait and just look at them. The evil angel is only about three feet away from me. It's roiling faster. I don't want to be distracted by it, so I choose not to look at it.

"What are you guys up to?" They both answer, "Nothing." They look guilty already. I lean forward, "Look, I can tell you're not going to tell me the truth so I'm just gonna lay it on the line. I'm gonna tell you a secret."

They both lean forward towards me. "You're being recruited right now, by the devil," I nod my head yes, as they both stare at me. "I don't know what you were just talking about, but I know it was very wrong and could hurt you both, eternally." I look from one to the other. "Do you understand me?" They both look at me nod yes, then look back at each other.

The younger one blurts out, "We weren't going to do it, honest. You won't tell anyone will you?"

The other one pipes up, "We're sorry."

"Remember," I point at the ceiling and whisper, "He's watching."

As I get up to leave, I realize the dark angel is gone. I breathe a sigh of relief.

I'm glad the danger is gone for now. I also realize they won't all be this easy. I want to talk to Zadok about my encounter, but I probably won't get a chance to see him alone until after lunch.

I head back into the counselor's dining room.

Seth asks, "What was that all about?"

"Oh, I just saw a couple of boys acting up. I thought I'd talk to them before they really get in trouble," I say.

After we finish breakfast, the rest of the morning passes with out any incident. Most of the kids are wiped out from yesterday's canoe trip so we just play fun swimming games.

After lunch, I look for Mr. Z. I'm beginning to feel confident that I can handle this talent God has given me. On the other hand, I fear I might not succeed on every encounter and what if the person is evil, not just the angel? Do I have a guardian angel I can call on? There is so much I don't understand. I know enough to know, I don't know enough.

Instead of Mr. Z., I run into Paige as I'm leaving the mess hall.

"Paige, can I please talk to you?"

Paige looks around to make sure no one is listening. She motions me to follow her. We sit down on one of the benches outside the chapel.

I wait for her to speak first.

"Look, I know I have to stop. It started out as a way to drop a few pounds. I just wanted to look good in a bathing suit," she grabs her middle, "and I always had this flab I could never get rid of. Girls used to tease me in the locker room about my weight. I just don't have the self control to stop eating, but I can control keeping it in my body."

"Paige, you are just so beautiful, it's hard to imagine you think there's anything wrong with you," I say.

"The problem is, I've been trying to stop, but I can't control it anymore. Whenever I eat, my body sends it back up. I can't stop it and I'm scared."

I reach out and give Paige a hug. Tears are welling up in her eyes.

"How long have you been doing this?"

"Since I was twelve. Almost four years now."

"Let's go together to Mrs. Timmons; she'll know how to find you help."

"No way. I don't want any adults to know. I'm too embarrassed."

"You just said you can't stop on your own, she can help you or find people who can. You have to try. I saw a show where this can eventually kill you. A hole can form in your throat, and you can bleed to death."

"Don't scare me," Paige says.

"This is serious, especially if you've been dealing with this on your own for four years." I take Paige's hand and start leading her to the main lodge.

She keeps protesting all the way but doesn't let go of my hand.

When we walk into the main lodge, I see Mrs. Timmons at the main desk.

She smiles up at us and says, "Hi girls, can I help you with something?"

"Can we speak to you in private?" I ask. She invites us into her office and closes the door. I'm in there just long enough for Paige to explain the problem, and then Mrs. Timmons asks me to leave. At least I did what I could.

I'm running late for my arts and crafts class, but it can't be helped. I hurry over to the classroom and I'm just in time to help clean up glitter;

it's everywhere. Tonight, for dinner we're grilling hamburgers. So with dinner duty there's not much to do except carry all the fixing's out to the picnic tables.

I look over to the woods for the dark angel. I'm to far away to see any details in the bright light. Zadok is working the grill so I don't get any alone time with him. A lot of the young boys still aren't back from a treasure hunt in the woods, including Seth and Robby's groups. I sit and eat one of the first burgers off the grill, before they get cold.

I decide to head over to the cabin to grab a jacket and a flashlight while it's still early and I have nothing better to do. As I approach, I hear giggling and crashing sounds coming from the woods behind my cabin. It could be the treasure hunters. I go inside and look for a flashlight. They never get left in the same place twice.

I catch a movement out of the corner of my eye in the direction of my cot. Strangely, it looks like my cot has its blanket tightly tucked in all the way around, not like I left it at all. I walk over and have to tug the blanket loose. Sure enough, a green snake. I pick up a small canvas tote empty it, and put the snake in. I sling my bag over my shoulder and put my jacket on. I remember to put a hump on my bed and tuck it in so it still looks like the snake is there.

I take the flashlight and casually stroll towards Robby's cabin. I make sure I see him and the guys down by the cookout before I enter. I place the snake in Robby's messed up sheets, taking care they look exactly the same.

I hope he screams loud enough so I can hear him. The thought makes me smile.

I run down to meet Seth at the campfire and ask, "How did the treasure hunt go?" Several of the younger boys start snickering and laughing. I just act dumb. Seth looks at me and smiles, "We had a great time, although my kids are still trying to learn left from right. They spent a whole hour going in the wrong direction."

Robby says, "We had sssssssuch a sssssssspectacular hunt."

I think to myself, not for the first time, Robby might be handsome, but not too smart.

"I hope you scream like a girl," I mutter under my breath.

Robby and his boys are to busy laughing at their inside joke to hear me.

After dinner, Zadok asks me, "Megan can you help me carry this stuff up to the kitchen?"

Finally a few minutes alone with him.

As we head up, he turns to me and says, "You did a good job today with those boys."

"I did okay, but they're not always going to be that easy to handle, are they?"

"No. They're not," Zadok answers. "You will eventually come across some that will need angel intervention and sometimes we get held up."[28] "Others need to be handled through prayer and fasting.[29] You won't win everyone either. It's not your decision."[30]

I tell Zadok, "One came to visit me in the middle of the night and put its hand on me. It really scared me."

Zadok just nods his head, "I can't protect you from seeing them and knowing they are there."

"On the canoe trip, it caused Charlie to break his arm. I couldn't move fast enough to stop it. What can I do? I'm feeling so useless."

"Okay, so you can't stop every bad thing from happening; so what can you do? What is within your power?" Zadok asks.

"Pointing out self-destructive things?" I answer.

"Good. You're on the right track. So the answer to the question, 'What does God want me to do?' is . . ."

"Remind them of what God says?"[31] I say.

"Yeah, sounds so easy doesn't it?" Zadok says.

"Megan, you will be walking a fine line between the natural and the spiritual. You have to remain firmly grounded in who you are. The dark angels are after you. They want to destroy you and any good you might do.[32] Stay away from evil humans that have a dark angel. The human part of them is too ignorant to be afraid even though demons tremble at the sound of His name."[33]

"Zadok, are you my guardian angel?"

"Not in the way you think. I've been sent to talk to you and encourage you for these few short days at camp. It's not for me to know or to tell you if I did know, what's going to happen when you get home. That's where your faith must be relied on. I do know that God sends us to be encouragers."

"So that means something is coming that I'm going to need encouragement for." My heart starts to sink. I'm not looking forward to leaving camp.

"Yes," Zadok answers.

"We still have a couple more days. Enjoy them while you can," Zadok smiles. "Remember you did have a victory today. Enjoy that. I do."

I leave the kitchen and head back to the campfire and Seth. I smile at him and he smiles back. I am going to enjoy what remains of this week. Everything else can wait until I get home.

*   *   *

That evening as Seth walks me to my cabin, we hear what sounds like a far off scream. Seth says, "Did you hear that?"

I try not to laugh, "I think that sounded like Robby."

"No, it sounded like a girl," Seth answers.

I burst out laughing. Seth looks at me and says, "You didn't."

I'm laughing so hard I can't talk, so I just nod my head.

I couldn't think of a more perfect way to end the day.

The next two days pass quickly. If anything, the dark angel seems to be avoiding me, every time I catch a glimpse of it, it either backs away or disappears. That dark angel knows I'm going to try to undo whatever damage he does. I'm not afraid of it anymore. Maybe I should be.

Seth and I meet up every chance we can these last two days, just to hang out. We meet at our special place every night to watch the bats and the shooting stars. We kiss, hug, hold hands, and give each other back rubs.

Zadok always sends Robby or someone to get us, whenever we get too romantic. He is definitely acting like a guardian angel.

\* \* \*

I can't believe today is our last day. Seth meets me in the dining room and gives me a big hug in front of everyone. The adults know it's our last day together so they don't say anything and look the other way. I get my coffee and bagel and he grabs his usual six doughnuts and a coke.

"I don't know how you can eat all that sugar and fat and stay so thin," I say.

"Fast metabolism. Besides I'm still growing. Coach back home says I'll probably grow 3 or 4 more inches."

I look at him and say, "I think I'm done. What you see is what you get."

He looks at me with powder sugar on his nose, "You're exactly what I want." "We're on for Bush Gardens later this month, right?"

"Absolutely," I squeeze one of his sticky hands.

I'm so glad Seth goes to a small private school so he doesn't have oodles of cute new girls chasing him. Most of the girls' at his school, he has known since kindergarten so they're more like sisters.

"You don't mind going back to texting do you?" I say with a hint of anxiety in my voice.

"Megs, you're everything I want, I mean that. I'm going to text you when I can. Otherwise I'll be studying, playing sports or hanging with Robby learning disgusting habits."

"Like burping the alphabet?" I say.

"Exactly."

"O.K. that makes me feel better."

I see Paige and excuse myself to go talk to her.

"Hi. How's it going?" I ask.

"Fine. Mrs. Timmons spoke to Mom. They've arranged for me to see someone when I get back home. She's a counselor who's had the same problem."

"Good. I'm glad things are working out for you. If you want to talk you can give me a call."

"Thanks. I don't know if I'm ready for that yet. I'm still kind'a embarrassed about the whole thing."

"Well, maybe I'll see you next year."

"Maybe," Paige says. Paige doesn't hate me, but she's not ready to be my friend either.

I walk off as some of Paige's cabin kids come up to her.

Seth and I head down to the beach for our last swim together. Mrs. Davis is walking around with a digital camera taking photos of everyone to post on our camp page. She takes one of Seth and me smiling in the water. I'm standing behind him with my arms around his shoulders looking over his shoulder. Its one of my favorite pictures. We look so happy.

While we're in the water, I look up and see the dark angel; it's decided to take on more of a human form. It almost looks like a shadow. It's not near anyone; it's just hanging out on one of the paths by the trees. I know that after I leave tomorrow it will still be here, looking to steal someone's faith. The worst part is there is nothing I can do about it.

Seth and I grab sandwiches for lunch and take them down to our place for the last time. Seth has his shirt off and I notice how handsome and tan he is.

"Wow I can't believe how fast camp went," he says.

"Yeah, I know. I'm going to miss you so much."

Seth puts his arm around my shoulder, "Me too."

I lean my head on his shoulder. Even after a swim, he still smells good. I close my eyes for a minute getting dizzy just on the way he smells.

We sit quietly for such a long time, that a small otter comes running across the rocks and under the dock, not even realizing we're here. He scuttles out and continues on his way.

"Wanna sneak out tonight and see how many shooting stars we can see?"

"Sure, I'd love too."

"Great 'cause I have a surprise for you."

"You do? What is it?"

"You'll just have to wait 'til tonight."

Seth goes to stand up and gives me his hand. "I think you'll like it."

"I like anything from you."

We walk back to reality. I have my last period of Arts and Crafts and Seth has his Archery; then one last dinner and one final night on the dock.

Later, while on my way to kitchen duty, I run into Zadok.

"Hey," I say.

"Hi, Megan come over and walk with me for a minute."

"I guess this will be my last meeting with you." I say. I'm at a loss for words. How do you say good-bye to angel. How do you say thank you? Does he even care?

As if he heard my thoughts he says, "You know angels have feelings too. I'm going to miss you. I hope we meet again. I want you to know, I will be feeling joy for every victory you have and sorrow for the losses."

I stop and give him a hug. He feels so human. "Thank you," I say, "you have helped me." I step back and say, "Maybe when I get to heaven, you can show me around." Zadok throws his head back and laughs. "Oh what a day that will be."

"Remember you are not alone. Maybe I'll be sent to help again. You never know. Don't try to fix things on your own, ask Him first." Zadok looks up at the sky.

"Zadok, that dark force is going to stay here, isn't it; but you and I are leaving. Who will be here to stop it?" I ask.

"The Lord's people and his word are here. That's enough," Zadok looks confident. "Good bye, Megan," he waves and disappears.

At dinner, Seth and I eat quickly and head out to the fishing dock. There is a bench at the end that we can sit on. We hold hands enjoying this time alone. Robby and Carrie join us on the dock.

"So what are you guys going to do without each other?" Robby says.

"I was hoping you could teach me how to burp the alphabet. That way I have something to impress Megan with the next time," Seth says.

Carrie groans, "Don't get him started."

"Maybe when Seth comes down to Busch Gardens, you could bring Robby and Carrie could come with me," I say.

Carrie says, "Really?"

Seth, says, "I'm sure my parents wouldn't mind."

Carrie says, "Really?"

"This is beginning to sound like a double date," Robby says.

Carrie says again, "Really?"

We all turn to Carrie and say, "Really!"

Everybody starts to laugh.

After campfire, I get the girls back to the cabin. Everybody's busy packing their stuff. I throw mine together quickly and pull Bri aside.

"I'm going out for a little while to say goodbye to Seth, can you get everyone to bed? I won't be too late. We're just going down to the old dock by the lake."

Bri says, "Well I do owe you one for putting that snake in Robby's bunk.

The memory of that scream is priceless. Sure, go for it."

"Thanks," I grab a flashlight.

"I'll see you guys later," I say to the Venus girls. They're so excited they hardly notice I'm gone.

I get to the dock before Seth. The moon is almost full tonight so I turn my flashlight off. Because of the stars and the moon, I can see pretty clearly. Bats are diving toward the water, preying on the flying bugs, hunting over the lake. I look behind me toward the woods for the dark angel, but he's either not there or blending in so well I can't see him. The waves are lapping at the shore in short rhythmic bursts. I hear the night sounds and wish I could spend every day in such a wonderful place. I feel so at peace.

I hear a step on the dock and turn my head to greet Seth with a smile on my face. It's not Seth. It's the dark thing. It's constantly moving, swaying, growing, and shrinking; and it's only about two feet away from me. Fear makes a stab at me, but I summon anger instead. How dare this thing try to ruin my last night with Seth.

"Leave me alone," I say loudly, afraid my voice will quiver or come out like a whisper. It stays, moving closer.

It speaks sounding just like I imagined a demon would, "We know you. Stop or we will destroy you. Stop, and we will go."

I hear moaning and deep guttural sounds.

I remember my flashlight and turn it on the creature: The light has no effect.

"You can't hurt me unless it is my Lord's will, Now LEAVE ME ALONE!" I shout.

I hear Seth's voice from the path, "Megan is that you, are you okay? Megan?" I hear him break into a run.

The creature looms over me and in more than one voice says, "We know you, we see you, we know," and then it's gone.

Seth grabs me, "Are you okay? For a minute there, I thought I saw someone with you and then I heard you scream leave me alone. What's going on?"

I fall into Seth's arms, shaking, and just let him hold me for a minute. Do I try to explain? This is not how I wanted our last night to be.

"There's no one here but me, I just got spooked by a shadow, that's why I yelled. I'm sorry."

"It's okay, Megs I'm here. You're shaking. There's nothing to be frightened of. Sometimes the moonlight can play tricks on your eyes. Have you been here long?"

"No. I feel silly. I love it out here and I feel safe with you," I hug him again and just stand there breathing in his scent. Shampoo and freshness, the smell of love and comfort. I guess I've made my decision not to tell him. Yet.

After our heart rates slow down we sit on the edge of the dock, leaning against each other.

"Remember I said I had something to give you?" Seth says into my hair.

"Yes," I say.

He pulls a ring off his finger, "I want you to have it."

"Oh, what is it?" I say as I put it on.

"It's my purity ring. I promise to be faithful and to wait for you. It's like giving you my heart. Please don't break it," Seth kisses me on the top of my head.

"Oh Seth, I love it, I love you," I think of what I can give him. The only thing I'm wearing is a gold necklace with my initial on it that my parents gave me for my birthday.

I say, "Here, hold my hair," I reach up and unclasp it.

"This is my heart to you," I fold it into his hands, "I trust you with my heart." We spend the rest of our time together watching shooting stars cross the sky.

The next morning, I rush to the dining room eager to see Seth again in the daylight. We hug again and take our breakfast down to the fishing dock. Today everyone is leaving within the hour.

"Do you feel better now, knowing that I'm serious?"

"Yes," I smile.

"Good. Then we can both concentrate on getting good grades so we can get into the same college together. And we can see each other on school breaks. There is a ski trip coming up on Christmas break that we can go on."

"My, now that we have all that romance stuff out of the way, you sound so practical," I tease.

"Well, one of us has to be," He says mocking me

"I'll call you as soon as I get home about the Busch Gardens trip."

"Are you sure your parents will be okay with that?"

"Sure, they trust my judgment and they want to meet you. They like your sense of humor from your texts."

"Oh, yeah, I forgot they read those things."

"Well they want to meet my mystery woman."

"I might need a drum roll for the big unveiling or should I just stick to the red carpet and the ball gown?" I joke.

"See they're going to love you," Seth smiles.

"Did I forget to mention my dad owns a rifle, and he might want to have you write an essay in 20,000 words or less on why you are worthy to date his daughter?"

"Hm, maybe we can work out some kind of deal."

The buses start pulling up to the main lodge signaling it's time to load up.

Seth and I hug a quick goodbye and he heads off to make sure his kids have emptied their cabin. I run up to grab my bag and check on my Venus girls one last time. We say good-bye to the Timmons and all the kids we've made friends with over the last two weeks. I wave goodbye to Paige. I stash my duffle and help Carrie load up the bays under the bus, then we get all the kids back on.

Mr. Steve does a head count.

I hear someone yell my name and step out the door.

It's Seth and he is kissing my necklace that he's wearing around his neck. I kiss his ring and we wave goodbye.

The drive back passes quickly. Carrie is all excited to tell me about the fun she and Robby had. Nikki tells me about the two or three boys she fell in love with during camp. She can't decide which one she likes better.

As we hit the main highway, I notice that a few of the cars seem to have a dark presence riding along with them and once, going in the other direction, I see a car with a bright light as a passenger and I smile.

My life has changed. For good or bad I'm not the same Megan I was eight days ago. I'm going home, but with what I can see now, I don't know how familiar home is going to be. I wonder if Mom and Dad are going to notice a change in me, and what about my little brother, Max? I wonder if I should tell anyone; and if I don't, how long am I going to be able to keep this a secret?

My best friend at home is Mandy. I've never kept a secret from her before. She knows all about Seth. How can I not talk to her about seeing angels?

She would believe me; but would it put her in danger? Would it put her immortal soul in danger? Am I just being weak and selfish wanting to share this with her? I have so much to think and pray about. I hope God is listening. Even more than that, I hope he feels like answering.

# Chapter Four

## Back Home

Mom and Max, my little brother, come to pick me up. Mom asks, "Did you have fun?" Why do Moms always ask the obvious questions?

"Of course," I say.

"Was that boy you like, Seth, there?"

"Yes, Mom," Max starts making kissy noises so I smack him and say, "Cut it out, grow up."

Mom says, "Don't hit your little brother," she pops the trunk for me to put my duffle bag in. So far, everything feels normal. I say goodbye to Carrie and give hugs to some of the kids before we head out of the parking lot to go home.

"Did you bring my cell phone?" I ask.

"No."

"Aw. I wanted to call Mandy and see what she's up to."

"You'll just have to wait till you get home, all of ten minutes."

"No Mom, we gotta stop for milk," Max says.

Mom says, "So tell me about camp."

I try to think of something she might find interesting that doesn't involve my relationship with Seth or Zadok.

"Oh yeah, Seth, Jackson and I got to save this girl from drowning. She went under and we towed her back unconscious and Zad . . . I mean Mr. Z. and I had to give her CPR and she's okay now."

"No way," Max says, "You're making it up."

"No I'm not," I say.

Mom replies while driving, "I'm sure your sister's exaggerating a little bit."

"No I'm not. Ask Mr. Steve."

Why do parents always think kids aren't telling the truth? My feelings are hurt that my own Mom doesn't believe me. They wonder why we don't come to them more often. This is exactly why I can't tell her about Seth. She'll just think it's some kind of puppy love thing and try to diminish the way I feel. I for sure can't tell her I see angels; she'd have me in counseling tomorrow and ground me for telling a lie.

Sometimes I hate being fifteen; it's such an in between phase.

Old enough to learn how to drive, but not old enough to drive by yourself. Old enough to like boys but not quite old enough to go on a date, one on one. Old enough to do all the testing for college, but not old enough to go.

Old enough to have a period and get pregnant, but not old enough to have a serious relationship.

I want to tell her about the Busch Gardens thing, but I think I'll wait until Seth calls. Maybe if Mom speaks to his mom, she'll let me go.

I try to think of something that will freak her out that doesn't include my seeing angels or demons.

"I put a snake in Robby's cot. He's a counselor, too. He screamed like a girl. It was so funny," Max starts laughing and making girly screeching noises.

Mom says, "Now why would you do that? That wasn't very nice. I hope they made you apologize to him."

I just shake my head. She just doesn't get it. I hope when I'm a mom that I remember what it's like to be my age.

As soon as I get home I text Mandy. We plan a call for after eight, then we have unlimited minutes and I can tell her everything about Seth and I, and she can catch me up on what's happened to her the last two weeks.

During our phone call, we make plans to go to the mall tomorrow. We both need clothes for school and our moms gave us a budget to do some shopping on our own. They're both busy with work and don't really have the time to take us anyway. The rule at my house is I have to show my mom the receipts for the things I buy. She can take back anything that doesn't meet with her approval.

Mandy says, "Wait till you see how I look, you're not going to believe it!"

I know she was getting her braces off so I say, "I bet you look beautiful."

At Mandy's house the next day, I knock. I have a smile on my face and I'm prepared to say how terrific she looks. When the door opens my jaw just about hits the floor. "Mandy, you are drop dead gorgeous! What have you done?" Mandy gushes, "I know, can you believe it?"

Mandy has her braces off all right, but it's more than that.

"My mom promised if I lost five pounds she would get my teeth whitened and take me to her hairdresser," Mandy says proudly, "and she bought me these new push up bras that make you a size bigger."

Mandy has always been pretty. But Mandy's mom is really into the bar scene and looks have always been the main thing in her life. Pretty just isn't good enough in her book.

"I've had my hair lightened with highlights, a new cut, my teeth whitened, lost the weight, and a new spray tan!"

"You do look gorgeous Mandy, but you've always been pretty," I say.

"Not like this," she smiles.

"You go girl, you enjoy it," I say. I'm happy to see her so happy.

"Now let's go shop."

We get in the car. Mandy is a year older than me, she was held back a year when she was younger, so she can drive.

Mandy is still gushing, "I feel like an ugly duckling who became a swan. I just know this is going to be my best year ever. I can't wait for school to start so everyone can see me."

"Mandy, you've always been pretty. You know there's more to life than how you look."

"Well, all I know is that I've had braces for the last two years and no boy has been that interested. You can say things like that because you have a boyfriend and you didn't have to wear braces. Now it's my turn to be the attractive one and have some fun."

Her remark stings a little bit, but she's right. I haven't had braces and I do have a boyfriend. It will be fun to see people's reaction to how fabulous she looks.

"Well now that you're going to be 'miss popular', don't forget I've been your friend in good times and bad."

She looks at me and smiles, "Of course not, we're M&M's. Mandy and Megan, the M&Ms."

"That's right, M&M's," I say.

We pull into the mall parking lot and grab a spot right in the middle. Even as we walk in, I see heads swiveling to look at Mandy. She's walking with her head held high and a natural sway to her hips when she walks. Mandy inherited that from her mother. I hope she hasn't inherited her mother's alcoholism. If she never takes that first drink, it won't matter. We go into all our favorite stores and try on all the new looks. Everything looks great on Mandy. We are having so much fun.

We stop at the food court for lunch. Mandy has a salad while I have Chinese and of course, a cup of Starbucks coffee.

Mandy says without me even asking, "If I keep the weight off Mom will keep paying for my tan and my hair."

I have no idea on how to answer that. My parents have never tried to bribe me in that way. I know Mandy's always kinda felt her Mother's love is conditional on her being the kinda of daughter Farrah wants her to be.

We always have to call her Farrah. Mandy's never been allowed to call her mom. Farrah doesn't want her boyfriends to know that she has a sixteen-year-old daughter and sometimes she even calls Mandy her sister.

Farrah had Mandy when she was sixteen, so she's thirty-two, but she tells everyone she's only twenty-seven. It's kinda pathetic. Oh well, you can't pick your parents.

After lunch, we head over to AE one of our favorite stores. As we're looking thru the racks Mandy practically squeals, "Look who's coming in!"

It's Alex and his friends Roger and Jason. Alex is a senior this year and Mandy had a crush on him our whole freshman year. Alex is on the varsity football team. He's very tall and handsome. He also has a reputation of kind of being a 'player'. Alex is the kind of guy who only goes out with a girl he can sleep with. Last year one of the cheerleaders went out with him and then he dropped her when she got too clingy. She was so ashamed she ended up transferring out of our school to go somewhere else.

As the guys come in the store, I see Jason nudge Alex and point to Mandy.

Mandy is busy pretending not to notice them. They casually walk up to us.

Roger speaks up, he was in my drama class last year, "Hi Megan, what's up? Who's your friend?"

"You know Mandy," I say.

"Oh, yeah Mandy. Hi Mandy," Roger motions to Jason and Alex.

"If you guys want to come, we're gonna build a bonfire out on the causeway tonight, it'll be fun. A lot of kids from school will be there."

Alex looks right at Mandy and says, "I hope you can make it. If you need a ride I could swing by and pick you up."

Mandy smiles at him and says, "Maybe Megan and I will meet you out there."

"Can I get your number?" Alex says.

"I don't know, can you?" Megan says flirting and then walks out of the store.

I say, "Bye guys," But they're not listening. They're too busy watching Mandy walk out. I walk out, hoping they're not watching me.

I catch up to Mandy around the corner and she bursts out laughing.

"Can you believe them?" Mandy says.

"Watch out for Alex he's definitely got his eye on you."

"This is so cool. Last year, I would have done anything to go out with him and now, he's flirting with me!"

"You're not seriously considering going out with him are you? You know what he expects from his girlfriends," I say.

"Yeah, I know. But it'll be fun to tease him if he's that attracted to me. It can't hurt to flirt with him."

"Do you want to meet them up at the causeway tonight? I'll drive." Mandy says.

"My curfew is ten o'clock. I might be able to push it to ten-thirty since it's still summer and it's my second day back."

We start heading out to the main mall exit. As we pass one of the stores, there's commotion with yelling, "Stop!" A security guard tackles a teenage Goth right in front of us. "Let me go man. I didn't do nothing."

"Yeah, then what's this?" The guard pulls a heavy gold chain out of the thief's pocket. "I didn't take that man. He musta' put it in my pocket, it was him!" The young man is trying to motion but the security guard is putting his hands in handcuffs.

"I swear I didn't take it, it was him, the guy in the jacket, over there!" The Goth guy says nodding his chin.

I look in the direction he's motioning. For a split second, I catch a glimpse of a handsome young guy, glowing black; and then he's gone. A dark angel. A dark angel right here in our mall.

"Don't worry, if you have an accomplice we'll see it on the tape. We'll get him too." The security guard hauls him away, calling for the police on his walkie-talkie.

I know no one else is going to show up on that tape. That dark angel set that Goth up. A sense of foreboding chills me.

Mandy turns to me and says, "Wow, can you believe it? This is going to be the most exciting year ever."

I think, Mandy has no idea how true those words are. If only 'exciting' were a good thing.

*   *   *

Later, that evening, my parents say I can go with Mandy but I must be home no later than ten-thirty. I draw them a map of exactly where we are going. I have my cell phone on me in my jeans pocket and I set it to vibrate. The rule is I have to answer it when they call so they can check up on me.

They trust me, but not everyone else I might meet.

Mandy comes in "Hi," she says to my parents and Max. She gives them each a big hug. "You look wonderful Mandy," Mom says.

"Thank you, Mrs. Laughlin."

"You girls have to be back by ten thirty," Mom says, "You're more than welcome to spend the night, Mandy."

My mom knows what Farrah, Mandy's mom, is like and chances are Farrah won't even make it home. She'll probably spend the night at her current 'boyfriends' place. Mom hates the idea of Mandy spending the night alone in her house.

"I brought a bag just in case you said okay," Mandy smiles.

"Good, go have fun. We'll see you later." We walk out the door.

When we arrive at the beach, I see a bunch of kids, most of who belong to the football & cheerleading crowd. Mandy and I mingle and talk to some of them. We wait around enjoying the weather. A nice breeze is blowing in off the water. Two wind boarders are out riding and jumping the waves.

A couple of people have even brought their dogs. As the sun goes down, some of the guys start piling the wood up for a bonfire.

Alex, Roger and Jason pull up in his car. They start unloading some logs and a couple of coolers full of drinks. They start piling on the logs and light them. Alex looks around and spots Mandy; he makes a beeline for her. I see her face light up even though she's busy pretending not notice that Alex is walking over. Mandy's talking to one of the cheerleaders about her spray tan. I'm just listening since I don't have anything to add to the conversation.

"You really should try out for the squad. If you can do a cartwheel and a split, I'm sure you'd make the team. You'd have my vote. You're so pretty you look like a cheerleader."

Mandy says, "Thanks, I'll think about it."

Alex comes up and says, "Well hello, I'm glad you came. Would you like something to drink Mandy, Megan, Susie? I've got sprite, coke and some beers, if you're over eighteen," he winks.

"We don't drink," I say, "But a couple of cokes would be nice."

"Cokes for the M&M's," "What about you Sus?" "I'll have a beer," she says trying to sound mature. As soon as he leaves she says, "I don't even like the stuff; I won't drink it, but at least I look like I do."

"Lots of adults don't drink; you don't have to drink to be mature," I say.

Susie just rolls her eyes at me like I'm the biggest geek in the world.

Mandy speaks up, "You know she's right, you've seen people get drunk and beer breath is disgusting," she says wrinkling her nose. I know Mandy's thinking of her mom.

"I guess you're right," Susie only sounds half convinced, "but I only pretend to drink it, okay?"

Alex comes over with our drinks, "Here you go ladies."

"So what have you guys been doing this summer?" Alex asks us, never taking his eyes off Mandy.

Susie starts telling everyone about her fabulous trip on a cruise, as one of the other football players walks up.

Alex pipes up, "Why don't you tell Shawn all about your trip; I need to talk to Mandy for a minute, excuse us." He gently grabs Mandy by the elbow and steers her away from us to walk with her alone down the beach.

I listen to Susie explain the details of her trip to Shawn, and then excuse myself. I walk over to the bonfire and position myself so I can keep an eye on Mandy and Alex. Alex has been nothing but polite; but I'm aware of his reputation. What they say about him, could be wrong.

One of the football team players comes up to flirt with me, but I let him know I have a boyfriend. He walks away to talk to some of the other kids standing around the bonfire. A play fight with several guys piling on top of each other breaks out. I laugh along with everyone else. When I look up, I can't see Alex or Mandy. I walk around looking for them. They're nowhere around. I look for Alex's car and realize it's gone. I can't believe Mandy would leave with him without telling me. I look at my cell phone, it's almost ten and I have to be home by ten-thirty.

I text Mandy where r u? No reply. If she doesn't show up in the next ten minutes, I've got to find a ride home or I'm grounded.

I start looking for a familiar face to ask, when I see Alex's car pull back into the lot. I see Alex walk around and open the door for Mandy to let her out. She waves to him and runs over to me.

Her eyes are shining, "He asked me out!"

"And you said—no?" I tease.

"No, we're going out Friday," She says.

I grab her hand and drag her to the parking lot. "You can tell me all about it on the ride home. We have to leave now to make it home by curfew. I don't want to start a new school year grounded."

"He's soo nice, he really listened to me," Mandy explains, "When he looks at me, I feel like he's looking into my soul. He's going to take me out for dinner and a movie on Friday. He wants me to try out for the cheering squad too. Alex said he would come take me to the tryouts. If I make the team, we could hang out together after practice. Aren't Susie and the other girls nice? Megan, we could try out together."

"No thanks, with my allergies I'd just be miserable, but I would come and watch you at the games. Besides, the practices would interfere with my writing for the school TV show."

"I told you we're going to have our best year ever!" Mandy looks at me with excitement sparkling in her eyes.

Mandy had no idea how wrong she was.

*   *   *

The next day, Seth's' mom calls to speak to my parents and invite Carrie and me on the trip to Busch Gardens. My mom gives her Carrie's number.

It looks like the trip with Seth is on for this weekend. I'm so psyched. Seth and I text each other excited about our last chance to see each other before school starts. They're going to pick Carrie and me up at my house by eight thirty in the morning. We'll get to the park right after it opens.

Mandy says, "I won't get to talk to you about my date with Alex."

"We'll just have to wait 'til after church on Sunday. Why don't you come over Sunday for lunch? We'll hang out. Paint our nails. You can tell me all about your date with Alex and I can tell you all about my day with Seth," I say.

"Okay sounds like a plan," Mandy says.

We head over to Mandy's to decide what she should wear for her date.

Mandy picks out a casual cotton summer dress with neon pink piping along the hem, neckline and arms and subtle light pink stripes running through out the dress. With her new figure, It's form fitting but high enough that no cleavage is showing. Modest yet sexy. It's perfect.

She picks out some white platform sandals. The white shows off her tan and the pink accentuates the highlights in her hair.

We decide on a mineral powder foundation and light pink lip-gloss.

Mandy is going to wear her shoulder length hair down and bring a hair tie just in case it's breezy out. I'm so happy for her. She looks beautiful.

"If Alex doesn't fall in love with you, he's a fool," I say.

"Where are you going to dinner?" "I think Frenchy's on the beach."

Frenchy's is a real popular seafood café on the beach. They have the best grouper sandwiches. I also love their steamed little neck clams.

"Alex says we're leaving early enough so we can eat, and then walk along the beach. We'll hit a late movie after that."

"Sounds perfect for a first date," I say.

I want to give her a warning about Alex's reputation, but I hold back. Mandy knows right from wrong. Besides, I would be upset if she were warning me about Seth. I know when to say no. The difference is Seth is a Christian who would never pressure me into having sex. He was raised, like me, to wait until marriage. The way Seth makes me feel: I know it would be wonderful to just give in and go with our feelings. Matter of fact I can't wait until we can go all the way. Sometimes I get dizzy just from hugging and smelling him.

I hope Alex is interested enough in Mandy to respect her.

Mandy and I break out the nail polish and give ourselves French manicures. They look classy and go with anything you wear. Plus, they're easy to touch up.

Farrah comes home from her work. She works as a nurse at a local plastic surgery center; this way she can get discounts on her botox, facial peels, and occasional nips and tucks. She loves her job. "Hey girls, clean up your mess okay? And run a vacuum would, ya? Mandy, honey, I picked you up some yogurts, fruit and Healthy Choice dinners. I have to jump in the shower and get ready for my date. He's taking me to that wine tasting thing in Tampa. You can reach me on my cell. Don't wait up."

"I better get going," I say. "My mom wants me to be home for dinner, wanna stay?"

"No. Alex might call; I'm going to wait at home."

Mandy drives me home. We say good-bye.

Friday, Mandy and I don't have time to get together. Her mom has off so they go to the salon together to get their tans touched up. My mom makes me baby-sit Max so she can run some errands without him.

I end up reading a book and texting Seth about what rides we want to hit when we get to the park tomorrow. Max manages to get peanut butter everywhere when I let him make his own sandwich for lunch. I spend about an hour wiping it off the floors, the fridge, the counters, the TV remote and the couch. It's even all over his clothes. He must have wiped his hands on his shirt and his shorts. Young boys are so disgusting. Carrie calls and we talk about what to wear for tomorrow. The day ends up flying by quickly.

That night I think about Mandy on her date. I hope she's having fun. It turns out the weather is beautiful for tonight and for tomorrow.

I wake up in the morning, right before the alarm goes off. In about a half an hour, I get to see Seth. I go in the kitchen and start a pot of coffee. I know my mom and dad are going to want a cup as soon as they get up.

Dad's an early bird but Mom's not. They both want to meet Seth's parents before we head off. I take a quick shower and get dressed fast. As I'm putting on my sneaks, I hear the doorbell ring. My Dad goes to the door and answers it. It's Carrie.

"Hey care bear," I say.

"Please don't call me that," She groans. Her cabin kids at camp had given Carrie that nickname.

"Okay, I thought you liked it," I say.

"Only at camp and only from ten year olds, then it's cute," Carrie answers.

"Oh that's okay, I'm sure Robby will think up something to call you by the end of today," I joke.

"What's Seth's nick name for you?" Carrie asks with a smile on her face.

"The love of his life or Megs, depending on his mood," I say.

The doorbell rings again. We hear Robby yelling, "Special delivery for Megan Laughlin, special delivery for Megan Laughlin. One over sized package with postage due."

My Dad looks at me and says, "That's not Seth is it?"

"No. That's his goof ball friend Robby," I say.

As Robby comes in, he picks up Carrie and twirls her around, "Hey super woman."

Seth comes in, "Cut it out, put her down," He says to Robby.

Seth walks up to my Dad and introduces himself, "Mr. Laughlin I'm Seth Wilson and this is my Mom, Dorothy and my Dad, Walter and my little brother, Sam."

My Dad does a comic aside to me saying, "I'm relieved. For a minute I thought Robby was Seth." Everybody laughs.

Robby says, "Hey, what's so funny about that?"

My Mom comes out with Max to meet everyone. After a minute of small talk, we're on our way.

Our goal today is to ride each roller coaster at least once and our favorites twice. Robby wants us to go on the flume ride so we can all get wet. We do rock paper scissors to find out whose ride we go on first. Of course, Robby wins. After handing Mrs. Wilson our cel phones, we go on the flume first, and we all get soaked.

After that, Mr. and Mrs. Wilson take Sam to go on his rides. They agree to let the four of us go on our own as long as we stick together. We're supposed to check in with them for a late lunch. Until then we head out to do our round of roller coasters. When get to the sky ride, Robby and Carrie go in their own separate gondola. Seth and I are alone for the first time since camp. Luckily, the ride stops when we're about half way across.

"I've missed you so much," I say grabbing Seth's hand. He comes over and sits on my side putting his arm around my shoulders.

"Me too, Megs. I've talked to my parents and they're going to let me come down with Robby for your homecoming dance, and then you can come up for mine."

"That would be great, then you can meet some of my friends like Mandy."

"And I can warn off the competition," Seth smiles at me.

We look down at the elephants and the passing people. So far, I've only seen two angels at the park, one good and one bad, neither of them close enough that I could do anything. The good angel had a human form, but the bad one didn't. I wonder why that is? I've only seen one in human form and that one only for a quick second at the mall.

"After that, we have Thanksgiving break and Christmas. I checked and both our church youth groups are going on the ski trip," Seth says.

"Wow, you've really got this all planned out," I say totally amazed.

We hear a loud Tarzan yell coming from Robby's gondola, "Me Tarzan you Jane." He starts hooting like a monkey at Carrie. Carrie's turning red. I can't tell if it's from embarrassment or because she's laughing so hard.

"I don't know how she puts up with him," I say.

"He's got her eating out of the palm of his hand," Seth says.

"Yeah, literally," we both laugh.

The ride starts up again and I give Seth a hug, inhaling the scent of his hair and his shirt. He smells and feels so good.

When we get off the ride, Carrie and Robby are waiting for us. Carrie says, "My face is hurting from laughing so much; you have to stop Robby." She play hits him.

"Let's go get some ice cream and see the hippo's," Robby suggests, adding seriously, "There's nothing funny about swimming hippos." We all laugh.

We go on one more roller coaster and then its time to catch up with the Wilsons for lunch. We head over to the Desert Grill where I get a coffee and a chicken Caesar Salad. Robby and Seth get these humongous corn beef sandwiches. Carrie chooses a turkey sandwich. We watch a stage show of Irish dancers and singers.

As we leave, Robby does a spot on imitation of the Irish dance and has us rolling in the aisles.

After lunch, we head over to the Egyptian exhibit. Robby runs into the gift shop, comes out and hands a gift box to Carrie, "I bought this for you because I think it matches the sparkling blue of your eyes, when you wear it, I know you'll only be thinking of me."

Carrie opens the box. Nestled inside is a necklace of an iridescent blue beetle bug encased in clear acrylic.

"How did you know I always wanted one of these? It matches my eyes perfectly," she jokes as she pulls back her hair for Robby to put the necklace on. "I'll treasure it always," she playfully bats her eyelashes at him.

We head on to the next coaster on our list. The day passes too quickly. Seth and I hold hands and hug each other while waiting in line for the rides. I don't think I've ever enjoyed waiting in line so much in my whole life.

On the way home, we stop at a fast food place for a quick dinner. Mr. and Mrs. Wilson are really great and Sam's okay too. Robby keeps every one in stitches the whole way home. What a great way to end the summer.

When the Wilsons let Carrie and I out, I only have time to give Seth a quick and public hug goodbye. I can't believe how fast the day went. I didn't even bother to look for angels most of the day or on the ride home.

The next morning comes too early, I'm happy to go to church, it's my first Sunday back since camp. Carrie's there too. I really didn't know her that well before camp, but after yesterday I can tell, we're going to become good friends. There is not an angel in sight. In a way, I'm kind of disappointed.

I was hoping one would show up that I could talk to or come to for advice.

I' m not comfortable talking to Pastor Bill about it, yet.

Carrie comes up to me after the service and says, "Wasn't yesterday fun?

I really do like Robby."

"Really? I hadn't noticed," I joke.

"Do you think he likes me?" Carrie asks.

"Carrie, I don't think Robby would have asked for you to come along or bought you that stunning necklace if he didn't. Didn't Robby tell you that he and Seth are planning on driving down to take us to homecoming?"

"He is? He didn't say anything."

"I think his humor covers up a little insecurity. Maybe he's afraid you'd say no or say something like, 'you don't feel that way about him.' "

"But I do. He's so cute and funny. How could any body not like him?"

"Well he is kinda high energy; I think he would wear a lot of people out."

"Not me, I think he's the greatest."

"Maybe next time you should tell him."

"I can do that."

After church, I call Seth. We talk about yesterday and make plans for when he and Robby come for homecoming. They'll both be sixteen so they can take turns driving. "You know Robby hasn't even asked Carrie to go."

"You're kidding. He musta' chickened out. He was supposed to ask her on the sky ride."

"I guess he was too busy acting like Tarzan," I say, "Tell him not to be afraid to ask, she'll say yes. Carrie's absolutely crazy about him."

"Or just plain crazy," Seth says.

"They kinda balance each other out, she can keep up with him physically and she enjoys sitting back, watching him be the center of attention."

We end our call with a promise to text each other later.

I call Mandy to find out how her date went with Alex, but after four rings, I am dumped into voicemail. My guess is she's on the phone with Alex. I know she'll call me as soon as she gets a chance.

Her date must have gone well or I would have received a sad face text or she would have called me right away. Only one more day off. School starts on Tuesday.

Later that afternoon Carrie calls me, "Guess what?"

I say, "What?"

"Robby asked me to homecoming!"

"And you said . . ."

"Yes!"

"Really?"

"Really," we both laugh.

"He was so nervous when he asked, it was so cute," Carrie says. "He asked me if I'm still wearing my bug necklace. I told him of course I am, until he replaces it with a vegetable or a mineral," we both laugh.

Carrie and I discuss whether we will end up in any of the same classes. Last year we didn't. That's one reason we didn't know each other well until camp. The only time we saw each other at church was at Wednesday night King's Kids and Sundays. Because we're teenagers, we often would be assigned to help the adults with different sets of the younger kids, so we never had a chance to say more than hi.

I'm kind of a geek so I take all the AP science and math classes I can, along with drama and TV production. Carrie leans more towards the easier classes, P.E., and she plays on the volleyball and softball teams.

We don't have much in common academically.

Oh well, there's always lunch. We agree to meet up at lunch tomorrow.

Mandy finally calls me back after dinner.

"Hey, how'd your date go?" I ask.

"Oh, Megan, Alex is so wonderful; it was the most romantic night of my life. Dinner was perfect; we went for a walk along the beach and watched the sunset. He kissed me just as the sun winked out. He was such a gentleman. Alex even opened the car door for me, and walked me up to the door after the movie. He even asked to meet my mom when he picked me up, but of course, she was out on a date. Afterwards he called me just to tell me what a great time he had. The things people were saying about him are just so wrong. We talked for hours and he explained everything to me. That girl from last year, her dad made them break it off; Alex didn't drop her. Her dad transferred her out of the school to keep them apart. Alex was heart broken."

Mandy keeps talking and I just listen, "I'm going to try out for the squad and Alex is going to stay for try outs and cheer me on. That way we can spend even more time together. He says he's never felt this way for a girl before. He thinks I might be the one for him. I'm so happy. I feel like I'm Cinderella in a fairy tale and he's the prince. Now I know how you feel about Seth."

"I'm glad you're so happy Mandy. He did seem like a nice guy at the bonfire, not at all like his reputation."

"Do you want to get together tomorrow, a last hoorah before school starts?" I ask.

"I can't, Susie and Alex are coming over to help with some cheering moves to help me make the team. Shawn and Susie are starting to date, so the four of us will probably head out for something to eat after. Farrah's excited I'm trying out for the team. She promised me a new designer purse if I make it. I'll see you at school on Monday though, O. K.?"

"Okay, see you then," I say. I'm happy for Mandy, but part of me is disappointed. I'm sure she'll make the squad, but that means less time for us. We've always been the M&M's, but now I fear this could be the beginning of us growing apart.

# Chapter Five

## Back to School

The first day is such a mad house. My Dad drops me off at the front of the school, I give him a quick kiss good bye; the windows are tinted so no one can see, nobody cares anyway. You can smell all the new clothes, books, and the excitement of the new year. Anything is possible this first golden hour. The pecking order hasn't been decided. There is still time for some kids to move up the social strata. Outcasts haven't been targeted yet. Even if you know you're low on the social order of things, there's still hope that others are lower. By your clothes, you can advertise which unspoken sorority or fraternity you'd like to belong to. Jocks, cheerleaders, designer clothes (rich kids and wanna-be's), Surfers, Skateboarders, Goth, Funky Drama, Druggies, Rappers, Band (carrying instruments), Eggheads, take your pick.

Teachers are out in the halls greeting their favorites and warning the troublemakers. Nobody has picked what table or benches are theirs, which restrooms are off limits to your social strata, almost every unspoken club has openings for the chosen few. Some of this will be decided by the end of the first day, the rest by the end of the first week after all the official clubs have had their tryouts and picked their leadership.

Broken hopes and dreams won't surface until next week, but everyone can enjoy this first golden hour.

I make my way to my homeroom. Mrs. Grey will be handing out our class schedule. I hope I don't get her for AP English. I had her last year, for some reason she doesn't like me. All the other teachers I had do, I work hard in their classes and I love to learn.

I'm pretty, but I'm definitely part of the Egghead club. Usually kids in my regular classes wait till I sit and then sit around me so they can try to cheat off my paper. I think it's funny. In a way, I'm happy people know I'm smart.

Mandy's smart, but her mother has made it clear that looks are more important. I'm sure Farrah is thrilled that her daughter is entering the ranks of the cheer leading social club. I just wish she would be as happy when she gets good grades. A lot of the cheerleaders are smart and pretty and some are very nice to everyone. I know Mandy will be one of those.

Mrs. Grey has assigned us all seats on a chart at the front of the room. She has left the last seat in each row empty in case we get new transfers in the middle of the year. I'm in a middle row next to the last seat so the chair behind me is empty. The bell rings and she hands us our schedules. Thankfully, I got all the classes I wanted, with all the teachers I wanted.

The year is starting off pretty good.

As we switch to go to our first class, in my case drama, yay, I notice a flash of bright light ahead of me turning to go into the band room.

Excitedly, I realize there is a good angel at our school. I stick my head in to see who it is. It's a boy I don't recognize. He looks Hispanic, tanned skin, dark hair. He catches my eye and smiles at me. I wave hi and smile back. The bell rings. I run for the auditorium. I know Mr. Shasta isn't going to be happy I'm late. He certainly won't believe I got lost since I live half my life in this class or the TV production classroom. After class, I have to run to get to AP microbiology at the other end of the school.

Next, I have AP chemistry right next door. Most of my kids in science class were in it last year; we all get along, we're all eggheads except for one cheerleader, Dawn. Dawn is one of the nice ones, she talks to everybody.

After chemistry is lunch. I look for Carrie, Mandy and the Angel.

I see Carrie at one table and the Angel going through the food line.

Carrie waves to me and I hold up two fingers asking her to save two seats.

She nods yes. I go through the line grabbing a chicken Caesar salad, and a coffee. I notice the Angel looking around for a place to sit.

I walk up to him and say, "Hi, I'm Megan, but I guess you already know that."

He smiles at me and says, "Hi, you can call me Johnny."

"Would you like to sit with me and my friend, Carrie, or are you waiting for someone else?"

"No, I'm not meeting anyone else today; I'd love to sit with you and your friends," Johnny answers.

He follows me to where Carrie is sitting. I make introductions.

Carrie says, "So how do you two know each other?" I just look at Johnny; I don't know what to say.

He pipes up, "I'm in band, next to the drama classroom," Johnny says. He takes a bite out of his sandwich.

The answer seems to satisfy Carrie's curiosity.

I ask Carrie, "How are your classes?"

"Fine," she says, "Only one teacher I don't like. Mr. B. I'm going to try and transfer out of his class into an easier one."

I turn to Johnny and say, "You must be new here this year. If you need help with anything, just let me know," I realize that must sound somewhat ridiculous to an angel since he can probably pretty much help himself.

"Thanks, Megan and Carrie. It's nice to know I have a couple of friends I can talk to," we all keep stuffing our faces.

"So where did you transfer from? Out of state?" Carrie asks.

Johnny barely looks up from his food and says, "Yes."

It's obvious he doesn't want to answer any more questions about his past.

Carrie takes the hint. Too bad. I was kind of interested in how he was going to answer.

I ask Carrie, "Have you seen Mandy or Alex?"

"They probably left campus to get burgers at McDonalds or something," Carrie suggests.

"Yeah, your right," I guess Mandy forgot she'd said she'd meet up with me at lunch. I'll have to wait for her to text or call me later. I saw on a poster board when I came into the school that the cheerleading tryouts are on Friday, so Mandy might be tied up till then.

It looks like we won't be spending much time together this year after all.

Before lunch ends, I tell Johnny, "If you need anything, I hang out in the auditorium or the TV production classroom. Also, here's my cell number." I write it down for him.

"Here write down your cell number," I say.

He looks at me funny, "I don't need one."

"Oh, yeah," I say. I'm still getting used to this whole angel thing. Besides, except for the glowing, he seems so normal.

I know I can't really talk to him in front of Carrie. Also, you never know who might be listening here in the lunchroom. The bell rings and we each head off to our next class. My next three classes are AP English, Algebra and TV Production/ Social Studies.

The rest of the day flies by with no surprises.

I see Mandy briefly as I'm switching to my last class. She has TV production the class before me.

"Hi Mandy."

"Oh Megan," she meets me in the hall, both of us carrying new textbooks from previous classes. "I'm sorry I missed you at lunch, it's kinda been a whirlwind. Alex has so many new people he wants me to meet. I'll call you later," she half skips and waltzes down the hall.

I try to not let it get to me, she is busy.

As I leave my last class, my cell vibrates. The window just says private so I have no idea who's calling. I answer my cell; it's Johnny. Later when I take it off vibrate and he calls; it rings to the tune of Handel's, 'Hallelujah Chorus.' I guess he has a sense of humor since that's not even a ring tone available from my carrier.

"Hi meet me over by the auditorium front doors. We can wait for your Dad there and talk. He's running a half hour late," Johnny hangs up before I can even answer. I walk over and sit down next to him. Kids are still getting on the buses and the ones who drive are milling about planning what they're going to do next.

"Hi, I'm glad you're here even if I'm not the reason you are here," he looks at me and says, "you're not."

\* \* \*

My face must of registered a hint of hurt because he quickly adds, "You are right, you're not the reason I've been sent, I'm sorry I was so blunt. I'm not used to this human form yet. It's been along time for me since I was called to serve on earth. I'm used to warring—elsewhere. Many battles are about to happen, and this is ground zero, for one of them. I can use your help. No. I need your help."

"What do you mean?" I'm beginning to lose that happy feeling that Johnny's around. Maybe it would be better if he weren't.

"I have experience on the front lines with this evil. I've followed it here. I don't have much experience with humans. This evil I've managed to keep out of the earthly realm till now," Johnny continues, "Let me explain better. It's like a killer who's been trapped by the police. Except he's been trapped in a crowded place. Pretend he has a machine gun and he's in a tower where the police can't reach him for a little while. He knows he has lost; it is just a matter of time before he is handcuffed, a few minutes before they reach him and stop him. But the gunman is mad. He is going to unload that gun and shoot and kill as many people as he can before they get to him," Johnny turns to look me in the eye.

"That is what is about to happen here. I've trapped him. I can't take him out yet. It is so hard to put spiritual things into this world, having to use words that can't quite get the right, true meaning across. We angels, exist outside time.[34] Time is part of your creation. What is happening here is really happening outside 'time'. It is like an iceberg, you can only see what is above the surface, but there is so much more below."

"Megan, you can help by keeping people out of harms way, steer them to what is right, if you can. Keep them out of his line of fire."

"The devil is a roaring lion, seeking whom he may devour.[35] Keep them away from the lion, Megan."

My Dad pulls up front to pick me up, "Who's that?" he nods towards Johnny.

"Oh, that's Johnny, he's new," I say.

"Should Seth be worried?" My Dad winks at me.

"Dad, no. Johnny has someone like I do. We're just friends."

"Where's Mandy?" My dad is so used to the two of us hanging together, of course, he notices she's not with me.

"She's driving now, has a boyfriend named Alex, one of the most popular boys in school, and she's trying out for the cheerleading team. I probably won't get to see her as much this year," I say. I try not to sound too sad.

I'm happy for her. I'm just blue that our interests are pulling us apart. The rest of the ride home, I pull out my phone and text Seth about my day. I ask how his day went. We spend the time before dinner talking the whole time. All in all, it was a good first day of school.

The next few days go fast as I get in to a routine. Carrie, Johnny and I continue to meet for lunch everyday. I get a role in a play and have after school rehearsals for that and our TV production weekly show.

At first, I keep looking around for the evil Johnny was talking about, but I can't see where it's coming from yet. I have no idea what I can do at this time to protect others. I pray about it too, but nothing seems to be happening.

That's what makes what happened next so surprising.

The next week of course, Mandy makes the cheering squad. I give her a big hug and congratulate her. A few days later Mandy run's up to me in the hall on the way to math class and says, "Guess what?"

"What?"

"Remember that Goth that got arrested for shoplifting?"

I look at her dumbly for a minute. Not expecting that kind of a question.

"The one right in front of us, the week before school? In the mall, Remember?"

"Oh yeah," I say. Remembering the glimpse I had of the dark angel.

"He committed suicide, last night!"

"No," I say. My stomach sinks to my shoes.

"Yeah, he left a note and everything. He posted it online. He blames some guy named Judas for ruining his life. How wild is that."

I knew about the dark angel, I had glimpsed him; I had even heard the Goth kid blame him, but I had done nothing. I should have tried to find out who the dark angel was. I could have talked to the Goth kid, tried to help him. Instead, I hadn't even given him a second thought. I'm sure this is what Johnny was talking about. "Keep them away from the lion."

Well, I've already failed once. I'll have to keep my eyes open so I don't fail again.

*　*　*

Two days later, there is a memorial service for Jordan, the Goth kid. Johnny picks me up first, then Carrie. When I get in the car, I can't resist asking Johnny, "How long have you been driving?"

Johnny just looks at me. Johnny's personality is so different from Zadok's.

Zadok had a sense of humor and gave off warm fuzzies. I don't know if Johnny is more serious by nature or if being human is so alien to him, he hasn't had a chance to learn. I decide to keep up the repartee to amuse myself, since it's not in my nature to be serious all the time.

"Couldn't you have asked God for a nicer car to drive?" I say to tease him. It's an older blue model. I don't know enough about cars to know what kind it is.

He answers, "Yes."

He waits a minute then explains, "I don't think it's important what kind of car I drive."

"I know. I was just teasing you. You really haven't picked up on the humor thing yet, have you? Knowing about sarcasm is kind of important if you're going to be dealing with teens."

He keeps his eyes on the road as he answers, "Not really, I can see the truth behind the words. The words themselves aren't very important. Most teens lie to themselves about what they're feeling. That I have noticed."

We pull up at Carrie's house and she gets in, "I'm not even sure I should be going. I didn't know Jordan well or any of the Goths."

I say, "We're going to show our respect. He was a classmate."

Of course, the other reason I'm going and Johnny's going is to see if we can catch the dark angel before he does anymore damage.

When we get to the memorial service, there must be around five hundred kids all milling about. Some of the girls are crying and hugging each other. I go up to some Goth girls who appear to have known Jordan well. I tell them how sorry I am and just listen. "I told Jordan to stay away from Judas, but he was just so fascinated by him. I could tell Judas was bad, really bad, not just pretending, and he could do some really creepy things."

I ask, "What kind of creepy things?"

She just stares at me then her face crumples, "Scary things, like hold his hand in a flame for a long time and not even get burned, talk in more than one voice, like he was possessed. Judas could drink a whole fifth of whiskey and not even get drunk. And move fast, like on the dance floor, I mean the strobes were going, but still to move that fast, I don't even want to think about it. I'm glad he's not here today. Maybe the cops will arrest him. I'm sure he killed Jordan, somehow," she starts crying again.

Johnny and I look for this mysterious Judas. He's not here today.

Johnny looks at me and says, "The battle has begun."

I know one thing for sure. Evil is here, in Clearwater, Florida.

# Chapter Six

## THe Battle Has Begun

Mandy and Alex have been dating now for almost a month. She's been so busy with practice and him that we haven't had a chance to hang out. This coming week starts football season so I'll get to see even less of her. So when she calls and suggests we spend Saturday together and asks if she can spend the night, I jump at the chance. When she comes over, I say, "So tell me all about Alex."

"You're so nice to listen, I know I've kind of been neglecting you, getting all wrapped up in this cheerleader thing and then spending the rest of my time with Alex. Thanks for being so understanding. I've never been in love before. Now I know how you and Seth feel about each other."

"So where is Alex this weekend?" I ask.

"Alex and his parents went to visit his grandparents. He'll be back on Monday," Mandy says.

I can tell she wants to say something, so I just keep quiet.

"Megan, you and Seth have liked each other a long time, right?"

"Well, we only made it official at camp, that's when he asked me to be his girlfriend and not date others. Why?"

"What do you guys do, I mean do you let him touch you? How far would you guys go? You know what I mean."

I show Mandy the ring Seth gave me. "I don't know if you know what this means."

"That's the ring Seth gave you, it means he loves you, it's a promise ring."

"Well, yeah, but its more than that, it's a purity ring. The most Seth and I will ever do before we get married is kiss and hug or hold hands, that's it. Seth took a vow last year that he would save himself for marriage as a sign of respect to his bride. Believe me I get dizzy when I kiss him and I want to do a lot more than kiss him. We have to restrain ourselves, it's not easy."

"How come you don't have a ring?" Mandy asks.

"My church doesn't do that ceremony, but I feel the same way. The great thing is Seth and I can have so much fun together and even have the sexual tension but not worry about STD's or pregnancy. I know it'll be great when we finally do 'do it', but we have a lifetime of that ahead of us, we don't have to rush into it."

I look Mandy in the eye, "Is Alex asking you to have sex?" I ask.

Mandy blushes, "Not yet. He wants to wait until homecoming so it's special. He's asked me to get on the pill. He says he has needs. And that if I love him, I will. He says that my future husband will want someone who's experienced and knows how to do it right and he'll teach me."

"If he's talking about you and some future husband, then he's not planning on being with you long term. It sounds like he wants to use you," I say.

"Alex loves me, I'm sure he wasn't thinking through what he said."

"I know how you can tell if he really loves you," I say.

Mandy looks at me eagerly, "How?"

"Just say, no sex till we're married. If he's willing to wait, then you'll know he really loves you. Mandy, you're worth waiting for. Don't sell yourself short."

"Look Megan, not everybody feels the way you do. My mom even offered to take me to get on birth control, and Alex's dad gave him condoms. We'd be careful. We're not stupid. Our parents are okay with it. Even the school gives out free condoms; they're okay with it too. They're not prudes. They think we're mature enough to handle it," Mandy says.

"Yeah well teenage pregnancies and STD's are at an all time high in teenagers and this is why. Just look at all the births to unwed teenage moms. What's so wrong with saying no and waiting?" I ask, "If Alex really loves you he'll wait. If he's so mature he should be able to control his urges, you're not animals," I say heatedly. I don't know why I'm getting so upset. Mandy's my best friend, I don't want her to get hurt by this guy.

"Remember, this is how Alex got his reputation last year. He had sex with that girl, let everybody know, and then dropped her like a hot potato. Don't let it happen to you."

"Now you're just getting mean. I told you what happened. That girl's father split them apart, not Alex," Mandy answers.

"That's what he says. He could be lying. All I know is if he really loves you he'll wait."

"You're the only one saying to wait. If his parents are okay enough to give him condoms and mine's okay to get me on the pill, then it must be all right. You can't expect everyone to wait until they're married. It's just not realistic," Mandy says.

"Well the reality for those who wait is no STD's, unwanted babies or abortions. I like my reality better than the one that includes those things," I say heatedly.

Mandy looks at me and says, "Don't impose your morality on me."

"If Alex and I decide to have sex, we will be careful. I don't want to talk to you about this anymore. We are going to have to agree to disagree on this subject. I always knew your religion made you a little uptight about things like sex, but this is the first time you've let how you feel come between us. I hope we can still be friends."

I feel miserable; not only wasn't I able to get across how important she is, but now she feels I've threatened our friendship. "Mandy, I love you. You know you're like the sister I never had. I just think if he Alex really loves you, he'll respect you enough to wait. I'm sorry I made you mad, but I'm not sorry for what I said. That's honestly how I feel."

The rest of our weekend together is kind of stilted. I can tell we both feel like we're walking on eggshells. Sunday morning Mandy comes to church with my family, and me but I can tell her heart isn't in it. I can feel her pulling away from me but I don't know what I can do to stop it.

Sunday afternoon, I feel relief when she goes home to wait for Alex's call.

Monday, at school, I say hi to Mandy, she waves at me but doesn't bother to stop and chat. Later, I over hear some of the cheerleaders talking about a party that someone named 'Jude' is hosting. Susie notices me listening and actually comes over to invite me. "Hey, Megan there's going to be this big party, it's at a warehouse that Jude has found for us to use. I know Mandy and Alex are going. She shows me a flyer she has. Rumor has it there's going to be alcohol and some other stuff so you might not want to go."

"Susie, who's Jude? I don't think I've met him."

"Oh, he's new in school; he's the most handsome guy in a tall, dark mysterious kind of way. You really can't miss him. He's getting to be very popular for a new kid. And having a party like this can't hurt," She waves and walks off to talk to some other kids.

At the time, I don't think much of it. I've never been one to go to the parties where there's going to be drinking or drugs. The next day, when my dad drops me off at school, we find graffiti, covering some of the buildings. The janitorial staff is busy scrubbing and pressure cleaning it off.

A rumor quickly spreads around the school that the kids who did it were caught; that one of the other kids turned them in. Later I hear the name Jude popping up. He's the one that turned them in and the video surveillance backs up his story. Jude is becoming a popular guy, with the kids and the staff. Later that day I go to the lunchroom, get my salad and sit with Johnny and Carrie. As I sit down, I hear a bunch of kids start to clap and holler, 'Jude, Jude, Jude'. I look to the door, and lose my appetite.

* * *

Jude is a dark angel. I feel Johnny next to me stand up. I reach out and put a hand on his arm to stop him.

Jude looks over at us and waves giving us a big grin. Next, he's surrounded by a large group of kids almost like he's a rock star. I excuse myself to go to the restroom. I feel ill that the dark angel has noticed me and saw me sitting with Johnny. I know I'm going to be targeted.

When I enter the restroom. I see a Goth girl crying. It's not a pretty picture; black mascara is ruining her carefully drawn face. It takes me a minute to realize it's the girl from Jordan's memorial service.

"What's wrong; are you okay?" I go over to see if there is anything I can do to help her.

"That's Judas, not Jude, His name is Judas," she sounds hysterical, "He's the one that killed Jordan, but nobody will believe me, not even the teachers. They all think I'm crazy. And now they think he's some kind of hero. What's wrong with them? Why can't they see him for what he is? Pure Evil. It's Judas without the makeup."

"I believe you," I gently hold her by the shoulders; she's so upset I don't think she heard me. "I believe you. I know the truth," I grab a tissue and try to help blot some of her makeup.

"What's your name? Mine's Megan."

"I'm Vania. It's short for Sylvania. I'm named after my grandmother from the old country."

"I don't know what to do. I know, he knows, I know," Vania whispers to me, "He's not human. He must be an alien or something. What if he's here to take over the world? I'm so scared."

I smile even though I'm scared too. I want to calm Vania down.

"Look I haven't told this to anyone, because I didn't think anyone would believe me. I'm trusting you with the truth. I know what he is," I say.

The bell rings for our next class.

"Look we need time to talk privately. Can you meet me right after the last bell, in front of the auditorium?"

"No. I'm too scared. Can I just stay with you?"

She looks like a total mess.

"Do you have an English class this year?" I ask.

"Yeah, English one."

"Okay. Come to my class, sit in the back, and I'll tell the teachers you're shadowing me for a report on an AP student. Okay?"

"Okay. I don't know if I can write my hand is shaking."

"Just do your best," I say. "You can do this."

"Now come on," I head out the door to English. Vania follows so closely she steps on my heels and bumps into my side a couple of times.

We get a few weird looks in my classes, but our story is so strange the teachers don't question it. Why else would a Goth skip her easier classes to go to other classes? If she were going to play hooky, she would have left school. I hastily wrote her a permission slip before we go into first class, but no one asks to see it.

Before next class starts, I call my dad to let him know I'll be running a half hour late so I have time to talk to Vania.

After we have our last class, I take Vania to the bench outside the auditorium. Usually Johnny's there to meet me, today he's not. Maybe he's sticking close to Judas/Jude.

"Do you ride a bus or something? I can have my dad give you a ride home when were done."

"No, I walk but I'm too scared, maybe I could spend the night with you?" She looks at me hopefully, "My mom works nights and Judas knows where I live. I've let him in before, when Mom wasn't home. I'm afraid if I go home, I won't be alive in the morning when my mom gets home." Vania blushes, "I used to like Judas in the beginning."

"Sure, you can spend the night, and you should be scared. You're right. He's not human," I tell her.

"Oh, I think I'm going to be sick," Vania runs to the bushes and pukes.

"I've made out with him. I was drunk."

"Vania," when she's done, I walk her back to the bench and make her sit.

I hunt in my purse and pull out some peppermint gum, "Here chew this."

"Vania listen, Jude, Judas, whatever his name is, is a dark angel. He is pure evil. He's here to destroy as many humans as he can."

Vania looks at me in disbelief, "He can't be an angel 'cause I don't believe in god. He must be an alien," Vania says earnestly.

"Look, that's probably why he's left you alone, if you're not saved, he doesn't have to try and steal you from God."

"So I'm safe, because I don't believe in god?" Vania looks at me like I'm crazy.

"No, you're not safe at all, but he's got time to toy with you because he knows where you're going when you die."

"You mean hell[36], don't you? You Christians can be so mean . . ."

"Vania, listen to me, you just admitted you know Judas is not human."

"I'm telling you what he is; I'm not making this up. The only way you can be safe is to accept you're a sinner[37], just like me. I'm not better than you; I'm a sinner. But Jesus died on that cross for us. If you repent and ask him into your heart you'll be saved.[38] Just like me."

Vania crosses her arms and looks back at me like I've asked her to jump off a cliff.

"Look Vania, we can go to your house pick up some clothes; you can spend the night at my house, but my family and I go to church on Wednesday nights, for Bible study. I want you to come with me."

Vania says, "Thank you, I really don't want to be alone tonight. I have to think about what you said. I know Judas isn't human, but a dark angel?"

"I feel safer around you," Vania smiles.

"Well don't. Until you make a confession of faith, your soul is in danger.

I can't help you if you die with out making that admission. If you're sure Judas killed Jordan, you could be next. When you become saved, God helps protect those that are his.[39] until then, you're not safe."

My Dad pulls up and gives me a look when I tell him, "Hi Dad; Vania is going to church with us and spending the night."

I've never understood the urgency of people becoming saved before. But now that I've seen Jude/Judas and know what happened to Jordan, suddenly it's all become real. Vania is in danger. I can feel it in my bones. Johnny's serious for a reason. A lot of people could wind up in hell before Jude/Judas is done. I know a lot of people are going to Jude's party this weekend and he'll kill them if he can. I have to try to stop him.

That night at Bible study, I see Vania calming down. When we have the altar call, she doesn't go up. She says, "I have some more questions first."

I say, "Okay we can talk tonight when we get home." I wish I knew my Bible better, but I just say a prayer and ask the Holy Spirit to give me the right words to say.

Later, that evening, after we brush our teeth, we sit down on my bed and her sleeping bag to talk. Somehow, even in bedclothes Vania manages to look Goth. Her pajamas are this black corset looking thing with long black silk pants so wide they hang like a skirt. "That's very 'bride of Frankenstein'," I say.

"Thank you." She twirls and smiles, "That is the look I was going for."

"Now what questions do you have for me, about being saved?"

"So Jesus is God, right, and he came to earth as a human, he died on a cross as a sacrifice for our sins; which is kind of gothic don't you think? Then if you say your sorry for your sins, and ask him into your heart, his death counts for you, right, 'cause he never sinned, right?" Vania asks.

"Yes. He died for us," I say. I don't want to confuse her by adding anything.

"How come it's so easy?" Vania asks. "Why don't we have to slit a wrist or cut off a finger or something? It sounds too easy."

"It's simple, because it is a gift to us. We have free will. We can choose to accept the gift of eternal salvation or we can deny it. God doesn't want puppets. He wants people who choose to love him."

"Here," I page through my Bible and find John 3:16. I point it out to Vania and give it to her to read.

"For God so loved the world that he gave his only begotten son that whosoever believeth in him, should not perish but have eternal life."

"Okay. I'm ready," Vania says.

"Ready?" I say.

"Yep. I'd rather belong to God than the devil. I've seen true evil and I don't like it. I choose to love God. Can you help me?"

I get down on the floor with Vania and take her hands in mine, "Dear Father in heaven, Thank you for the gift of your son, Jesus Christ" I look at Vania and say, "repeat after me."

Vania says, "Thank you Father in heaven for the gift of your son Jesus,"

I say, "I am sorry for my sin, please come and live in my heart today."

Vania repeats it.

We both say, "Amen."

"Okay. Your soul is safe as long as you believe."

The house phone rings. My dad yells from the kitchen, "it's for you Vania."

Normally, my dad would not put through a call this late at night but because it's for our guest, I guess he's making an exception.

My Dad brings the phone to the door and gives it to me.

Vania turns pale, "I know it's him, Judas."

I immediately put it on speakerphone.

We hear a deep-throated chuckle, "I know what you're doing with your new little friend."

"Leave her alone, she's not yours anymore," I say.

"Judas scores 1 with Jordan, Megan scores one with Vania. Looks like it's a tie score. Let's have a tie breaker, how 'bout my party Saturday night? I'll bring the alcohol and the drugs; oh, and you can bring your Bible."

Judas/Jude lets out a deep guttural laugh and he's gone.

Vania is shaking when I hang up the phone.

"It's okay, he can't hurt you anymore as long as you rely on your faith."

"I know, I just can't believe how close I was to evil and I didn't even know it. I was so confident that I was in control of me and the decisions I was making."

"But you made the right choice. You're okay now."

Vania looks at me in fear, "What are we going to do about that party Saturday night? How do we stop people from getting hurt?"

I look at Vania, "Do you trust me?"

"Yes," she says.

"Do you believe Judas is a dark angel?" I ask.

"Yes. I mean it's so obvious now."

"Do you wonder how I know he's a dark angel?" I can tell by the way her eyes widen that she hadn't thought about how I would know.

"For some reason God has given me the gift to see good and bad angels. When I look at them, they appear to be glowing. Good ones glow light and the bad ones glow dark." I continue, "You are the only person I've shared this with. You are the only one, and only because you could tell Judas wasn't human."

Vania looks at me and nods her head, "Wait, you said good angels glow white that means you've seen one of those too! Can you get a good angel to help us fight Judas?"

"Yes. I think he's here to fight Judas."

"Let's call him," Vania says handing me the phone.

I take it from her and put it down. "It doesn't work that way. He's a messenger of God. He's here to do God's will, not ours."

"Well can we pray to the angel to get him here?" Vania asks.

"No. The angels are creations of God, like us. We don't pray to things that are created, they can't help us. Also, that makes them into idols by thinking they have the power that only God has."

"Oh," Vania says. Her face brightens with a smile, "I know why God picked you! He picked you 'cause you understand these things."

"Maybe," I say, "What we can do right now is pray in Jesus' name for him to send us help. We don't want to face Judas on our own."

"Let's do it," Vania says.

Thursday morning, My Dad drops Vania and me off. Mom, Dad and Max had given me quite a few inquisitive looks over dinner last night when I brought Vania home with me. They treat Vania like family and even enjoy bringing her to church. I think their curiosity was sparked over how I had met Vania, because as far as they could tell, we don't have anything in common.

Vania and I still aren't sure how we are going to handle Saturday.

"We could call the cops once the party is underway." I suggest.

"All Judas will do is give the kids another location to meet up at and a ½ hour later, the party will be going strong so that won't work." Vania replies. She adds, "I know 'cause a month ago I was hanging with Judas, remember?"

"Oh, yeah," I might be book smart, but I'm awfully street dumb.

"First, we decide we have to have one of the kids give us directions on how to get there," Vania says.

I know it's in an industrial park somewhere, but that doesn't narrow it down much.

I didn't get around to telling Vania that Johnny is the good angel. She never asked, so I guess she assumed the angel wasn't a student.

Judas, who is now Jude, is hanging with the football cheerleader crowd.

I can't get any of my new friends in that group to speak with me.

I hear one of them call me 'snitch.' Later I see Jude pointing me out and it's clear he's turning them against me with rumors. There's no way Vania, a Goth, is going to be able to get in with that crowd either.

I tell Vania to meet Johnny, Carrie and me for lunch. I have one more idea I can try out.

I go to the registrar's office and show her my student I.D. and my TV production badge. "Hi, I'm Megan Laughlin, and I'm doing a story on how hard it is for transfer students to assimilate into a new school. Especially for those who start a couple of weeks later. I need a list of the students who came in a week or two late to interview for the story, and can you include their picture from their student I. D. so I can find them?"

"Sure, sweetie, but the picture can't leave the office. It'll just take a couple of minutes." The registrar goes to her computer and looks up her records. "Well honey, it might not be much of a story, it looks like we only have five that started after the year began, but good luck."

She hands me two print outs, one with their names and one with their photos. I glance at the photos briefly, but Jude/Judas doesn't stick out so I look at the names. There isn't a Jude/Judas listed. I read through the names again. Nope. I look back at the pictures more carefully this time.

There he is. I have to do a double take. In the student photo, he has long blonde wavy hair. He looks like a surfer dude. And his name isn't Jude or Judas. His name is Damon Vincent Lawless. His initials are DVL.

I guess Damon likes games. Now as Jude, he wears his hair brown and just past his ears in a preppy look. His eye color is different too. In the photo, his eyes are brown. But, as Jude, his eyes are a startling light grey blue and very magnetic. Jude definitely has the magnetism of a rock star. In the picture, none of that comes through, he looks washed up.

For a minute, I think about asking for an address, but then I realize that would be as phony as any name or look he chooses to go by. He can appear to be any human form he desires to suit his purpose. First, he was a surfer, then a Goth, now a prep. He's been at his evil purposes a long time.

A month ago, I knew creatures like him existed, but I never imagined they really affected my life in any way. Now I know how wrong I was.

This is real and this is my life.

Johnny, Vania and Carrie are already at the table when I arrive. Vania isn't shy and has introduced herself as my new friend. Our little group is growing. I had warned Vania not to say anything unless I bring it up. I still haven't told her Johnny's an angel and of course, Carrie has no clue as to what is going on since I haven't told her anything.

I might not be able to talk privately to either Johnny or Vania today, since I have to leave right after school, eat a quick dinner and come back for my TV production club meeting. I wish I could tell Johnny and Vania about Jude/Judas also going by the name Damon. I'm not sure what I should do and really need Johnny's advice. The bell rings signaling the end of lunch.

Later, I wish I had ignored the bell and talked to Johnny. Maybe things wouldn't have ended as badly. Maybe.

# Chapter Seven

## Angel in the Shadows

Tonight, I have a meeting for our TV show, which runs live on Friday. The meeting is running at least an hour late, with all the bickering between Emma and Clint on who is going to be the on-air talent for each story. They're acting as if it is a matter of life or death. Finally, I suggest they do rock, paper, scissors for the lead story and the loser can do next week's lead. Mrs. Hixon our advisor has already left, as she was late for picking her son up from soccer practice. All we have to do is lock up before we leave. Clint and Emma walk ahead to the parking lot where our parents are waiting to pick us up; I ask them to let my mom know I'll be out in a few minutes as my bladder is about to burst.

It is dark outside. Leaving the building, I can see the glow from car headlights bouncing off the buildings in eerie patterns of light. The outside overhead lights are still off. They haven't been reset for it getting dark this early. The science building blocks my view of the parking lot, so I stop and wait for my eyes to adjust to the darkness. That's when I sense, off to my left, movement. I look over and see in the shadows the glow of a cigarette. I feel drawn toward the glow to find out who's there. My heart starts to race as the stranger steps into a pool of light leaking from the building doors.

My heart sinks as I realize it's Jude/Judas/Damon.

He's as handsome as usual but I can feel his hatred rolling over me like waves in the ocean's surf. It takes all my strength not to take a step backward from the heat of his anger. I can see he's barely in control, but I know he can do nothing to hurt me without God's permission.

I want to run toward my moms' car and safety, but then I feel foolish for not having the courage to face him. I boldly walk toward Damon and try to think of what to say. Saying hi seems too ordinary, friendly and dorky. Confronting him feels dangerous.

Before I can speak, he turns to me, tilts his head away to blow out smoke and offers me a ghost of a smile. He speaks menacingly, "What—do—you—think—you—could possibly say—to—me?" pausing between the words.

Damon's superiority and disdain for me are dripping from each accentuated word.

My heart sinks as I realize I'm playing right into his hands. His meeting me tonight is intentional. Damon was waiting for me. He's not pouring on the charm the way he does for everybody else. Damon doesn't have to maintain a façade for me. I realize now that all he wants to do is destroy me and every other mortal who happens to gain his attention. I'm disappointed and angry with myself for wanting him to be charming, so I blurt out, "I know what you are, Damon. I'm going to stop you."

He looks down at his feet and takes another drag off his cigarette before he answers, "All men are like grass

And all their glory is like the flowers of the field

Grass—withers-

And the flowers—fall,"[40] with this Damon knocks his ash off his cigarette.

He looks at me and continues, "I am the predator and you the prey, mouse," he moves slowly closer,

"I am a roaring lion seeking whom I may devour."[41] Damon takes a step towards me, and crushes his cigarette.

I'm afraid to stay but more afraid to show my fear, so I stand my ground. I know he's quoting scripture, but my brain is paralyzed just thinking about how fast, and strong angels are. The only thing I can hang onto right now is my faith that God is protecting me, since I can't even speak.

"I'm asking to sift you, mouse."[42] He whispers in my ear. I can smell the cigarette smoke lingering on his clothes.

He looks down at me and before I can react, he bends down with supernatural speed and kisses me on the lips. His lips are cold and burning. He presses them against mine so fast, my lips are instantly bruised. There is nothing sensual behind his façade. At the same time, he puts his hands on my ribs and squeezes so hard it takes my breath away. He stops the pressure just short of my rib's cracking. It's an attack, he means to hurt and destroy me. All this hits me within a heartbeat. I break free and run as soon as I'm aware of what's happening. I look back over my shoulder, when I'm safely in the parking lot. He's gone.

Damon's kiss was an attack on me. He meant to scare me by showing how much faster and stronger he is. I'm so angry with myself for even letting him get close enough to do that. What was I thinking? Keep evil far away.

Damon was right, I have nothing to say to him; I need to avoid him and just concentrate on keeping others away also.

Friday morning we have homeroom, I only have to stay five minutes to check in and then I get to go to TV production to help run our show.

I get to class and stop dead in my tracks. Judas/Jude/Damon is sitting in the chair behind mine.

Mrs. Grey says, "Megan have you met Jude? He's new to the school these last two weeks."

Mrs. Grey assigns her students alphabetically. My last name is Laughlin, his is Lawless. My heart sinks. He planned this all along.

I look at her and say, "I have to get to TV production," and run out the door. There's really not much she can do about it today, because she knows it's true.

After homeroom, I get to my science class. I'm feeling a little better because we only have homeroom a few times a semester. I can handle that. Microbiology is one of my favorite classes. I love the experiments.

This year we have an odd number of students; so Mrs. Mack asked if I would mind not having a lab partner, which is fine with me. I'm reviewing my notes when the bell rings so I don't look up till she begins to speak. To my horror, Damon is standing at the front of the class. Not again. This can't be happening. School is turning into a nightmare.

"Class it looks like we have another gifted student joining us this semester. They've moved Damon," Damon interrupts, "Ma'am I prefer to be called Jude, after my Father."

Mrs. Mack continues, "Oh, alright, Jude. They've moved Jude up from his regular classes into AP because of his high test scores."

"Megan back in seat c-six will be your lab partner; if you will kindly sit next to her in c-five. Thank you."

I try not to look at him. I can't believe this is happening. Damon sitting next to me everyday; my situation fills me with anxiety. I made up my mind to avoid him and now I'm put in situations where it's not even possible. I hope Johnny's at lunch today. I need some advice. I need moral support. I don't think my year could get much worse.

I am wrong, so wrong.

At lunch, Johnny and I are the first ones at the table. I only have a few minutes before Carrie and Vania join us, so I launch right into my concerns. "What am I going to do? He's latching himself unto me and ostracizing me all at the same time."

"Don't worry; it's going to get worse first," Johnny says. I look at him like he's crazy.

"Seriously, don't worry. Worrying will only hurt your faith.[43] Second, keep praying, and ignore him. He might get tired of you if he's not getting the reaction he wants."

"Okay, I can do that," I say. At least now I have a plan of action.

"Should I tell Vania or Carrie about you?" I ask.

"Yes on Vania, she might need my counsel since she's just a baby Christian. Not yet, on Carrie, the timing's not right."

"Okay, thanks. What about the party on Saturday?" I ask.

"We'll go. I'll pick you and Vania up at seven o'clock tomorrow night. Bring a Bible," Johnny answers.

"That's funny, 'cause that's exactly what Judas said to bring."

After lunch, I find out Damon's also in my algebra class. At least this time I'm prepared. I totally ignore him. At least he's only in two of my classes and home room. It could have been worse. It could have been all of them.

Out of nowhere, my cell phone rings. My teacher, Mrs. Abbot says, "Hand it over. Please get your parent to see me to get it back." I look at the phone # to see who called. There's no number in the window, just the words, 'C U @ Party.☺'

Great. We technically aren't allowed to have cell phones on us. The teachers are okay with them as long as they're turned off during class and out of sight. Mine was turned off. Obviously, Jude/Judas/Damon has a few tricks up his sleeve. Even if I take the battery out, I'm guessing he could still make it ring. I guess, in the future, I'll have to leave it in my locker.

I fold my hands and start to pray. I pray for protection, peace and strength. Mrs. Abbott goes over a couple of concepts on the board and writes down some sample problems to work on in class and for home-work. I copy them down and continue to pray. I can do my homework later. I'm going to be grounded tonight anyway, after the prank Damon pulled, so I'll have plenty of time to get it done. The rest of the time, I plan on reading my Bible and praying; it's really the only defense I have. The only way I can get to Damon.

About a half an hour into praying, I look over at Damon. He definitely looks uncomfortable. I go right back to praying and try to forget about him.

After school, I meet up with Johnny and Vania.

"I only have about five minutes before my Dad gets here and I'll probably get grounded, so Vania, Johnny is one of the good angels I told you about."

"No way," Vania says.

Johnny looks at her and deadpans, "Way."

"Wow."

"Any way, you two might have to go to the party alone tomorrow night. I'm sure I'm gonna be grounded. Damon/Jude/Judas made my cell ring during class."

Vania looks at me, "Wait a second, information overload. You're saying Judas is calling himself Damon now? Not to mention Johnny's a good angel."

Johnny looks at Vania, "Look, I have to talk to Megan's Dad when he gets here. Then I'll give you a ride home and we can talk. Since you're a fairly new Christian there are some things I want you to be prepared for and other things I want you to avoid and pray about."

Vania just looks at Johnny in shock, "You look so normal."

"Do you want to see my wings? That's a joke," Johnny says.

Vania chuckles nervously.

"That's alright, maybe later," Johnny answers. Now neither of us knows if he's joking or not. Vania looks at me and I just shrug my shoulders. Except for him glowing, I've never seen anything else of his spiritual nature.

My Dad pulls up. Johnny opens the door.

"Hello Mr. Laughlin," "I'm Johnny. Megan had her cell phone confiscated by a teacher today after it rang in class. I forgot about the ring function. I'm sorry sir."

I stand there in amazement. Technically Johnny didn't lie. He does have the power to turn the ringer off.

My Dad turns off the car, looks at Johnny and says, "That's okay son, we all make mistakes. So Megan who do we go see to get your phone back?"

We all head over to Mrs. Abbott's classroom and get the phone back. Johnny even apologizes to her for the class being interrupted.

She accepts his apology graciously and gives my Dad the phone.

Before we know it, I'm on my way home with Dad and Vania is getting a ride home with Johnny.

That evening I text Seth, and do my homework. I'm nervous about the party tomorrow night. I stay up later than I should, playing out different scenarios in my mind of all the things that could go wrong. I really don't want to go. But lives and souls are at stake. I remember watching this show about street evangelists who go to New Orleans during Mardi Gras, talking to people about salvation on the street corners and how most of the people walking by treat them like kooks. I imagine what those Christians feel like.

I'm thankful Johnny is going to be with us. He's a show of God's strength. A physical reminder that we are not alone.

I pretend I'm telling my parents the truth. "Bye Mom and Dad, just going out to battle some dark angels and save some souls. See you later."

That makes me laugh. The phone rings and I jump.

I pick it up, "Hey it's Vania."

"Hi."

"Johnny wants you to dress Goth for tomorrow night. I guess word has gotten around to beat you up if you are seen anywhere near the Rave. They already have a backup place scheduled in case you tell the cops. If we dress you up, do the makeup and the hair color, you'll pretty much be invisible."

"Okay," I say.

Vania continues, "I also got us some glow in the dark pacifiers and jelly bracelets so we'll blend in. Don't worry I'm coating the bracelets with superglue so they're really strong."

"I have no clue what you're talking about. It's like your speaking a different language," I say.

"I know." I hear a heavy sigh. "The pacifiers mean you're into ecstasy, that's a drug, some of the kids' just suck on lollipops. The glow sticks, same thing." Vania continues, "The jelly bracelets stand for which sex acts you're willing to do. It's all a big naughty game. Some of the girls even wear lipsticks to show what they will do."

"I'm not wearing the bracelets," I say. I draw the line at that.

"Okay. No problem. Well just say you have a boyfriend."

"I do. His name's Seth. He lives up in Jacksonville," I answer defensively.

"Okay. Okay. I forgot to ask Johnny how far undercover. I guess some of it is a little too far," Vania says.

"Johnny did say we should get together early tomorrow, so I can clue you in on some of the hand signals. It's so noisy in these places that there's a kind of code. We'll make up some of our own too."

Vania decides to come to my house tomorrow around noon. She'll either catch a bus or have her mom drop her off.

Saturday morning, I get up and get started on my chores first thing. Feeding the pets, unloading the dishwasher, vacuuming and dusting the house. I throw my dirty clothes in the laundry room. I'm all set by the time Vania shows up. I wonder how I'm going to explain my new look to my Mom.

Vania says, "You write reports for the school TV show. Tell her you're doing a report on the life of a Goth."

I feel stupid, "Oh yeah, that makes sense."

Vania comes equipped with a big military duffle bag. She's cool and confident today. The first thing we work on is my hair. Vania takes out a bottle of 'spray on' pink hair. She sprays it on then teases my hair and puts in some hair gel. She teases it again on to the top of my head. Vania gets out a ponytail holder and ties it on top of my head. Now I'm sprouting a waterfall. She teases and gels my hair some more to get a few spikes sticking up and out of my waterfall, then hits my hair again with the pink spray. She opens a jar of glitter, mixes it with the hair gel and glitters my spikes. Vania then takes a metal ring and puts it half in and half out of my nose. She presses it a little to hold. Now I look like my nose is pierced.

I barely recognize myself. We try on some of her clothes and settle on one of my pink tops ripped in the right places by Vania. She layers a chain mail looking necklace that almost covers my whole front. I finish up with one of her black skirts and ripped fishnet stockings. The skirt is one of her longer ones she wears to school, not the short skirts she wears out clubbing. We finish with a pair of my black sneakers. She has a long metal chain for a drooping belt that I have to pin in place. She has several oversized safety pins that she positions in the right places.

Next, Vania gives me metal bangles for my arms and rings for my fingers. She also paints my nails black. Finally, the only thing left is my makeup.

Vania helps me to put on fake eyelashes with diamonds. I feel like I'm wearing spiders over my eyes. She does a Cleopatra look on my eyes using black and hot pink. She adds a little black to my checks and lips.

I don't recognize me at all. I practice moving the way Vania teaches me and some of the facial expressions and dance moves.

"Some last advice, don't drink anything anybody offers, GHB the date rape drug is odorless and tasteless. Bring your own soda or water in a bottle with a cap. Don't ever set it down and leave it alone. It's better just to wear it or wait."

Vania herself is wearing an old-fashioned metal canteen. At first, I had mistaken it for a purse.

We eat a quick dinner of frozen pizza that I stick in the oven. I doctor it up with some extra cheese.

My Mom gets home from shopping and sticks her head in the kitchen. "Can you girls tell Megan I' m home."

I look right at her and say, "Sure." She leaves the room and we burst out laughing.

I get up from the table and say, "Mom it's me!"

"Megan, what are you doing?" My mom's look of shock is priceless. No wonder some kids rebel if this is the reaction they get, it's kind of cool to be able to shock the parents who think they know you so well.

"I'm going to write a report on what it's like to be a Goth for a night," I say, "Can you take a picture of me to go with the report?" I think I may as well turn this experience into a homework assignment. I can kill two birds with one stone.

Mom gets her camera and takes a picture of me and then one with Vania.

"I'm glad your Dad isn't home to see this. Try not to give him a heart attack if he gets home while you're dressed like that tonight." Dad had taken Max to a Karate tournament; they probably won't be home until after us. My curfew is still ten-thirty, which Johnny knows.

Johnny pulls up at seven o'clock, on the dot. We load into his car. Vania sits up front and I kinda cower in the back. I've never not been welcome somewhere before so this is a new experience for me. I've brought my King James Bible and my NIV King James version. I tell Johnny, "I wasn't sure which one you'd want. Old English or new."

"Actually I was hoping for the original Greek, Latin, Aramaic and Hebrew." Johnny sounds disappointed.

I start to apologize when he turns around to look at me and says, "I'm joking."

"You're getting better at the humor thing," I say.

"Do you know where you're going?" I ask, as Johnny winds through a neighborhood.

"Yes."

Johnny pulls up about a block away from Mandy's house.

"Oh, I get it; we're going to follow Mandy and Alex."

Johnny and Vania answer together, "Duh."

"I see you've been picking up some slang and teenage angst from Vania."

Johnny and Vania look at each other again and say, "Duh."

"Okay. Okay. What exactly are we going to be doing tonight?"

Johnny speaks up, "You and Vania are going to try and save anyone who might be close to O.D.'ing on drugs or alcohol. I'm going to try and stop Judas from harming anyone. If he tries to approach you or hurt you, I want you to start chanting, 'Judah' over and over, as loud as you can. See if you can get the crowd doing it."

"Why?" I ask.

"Because in the Bible, God would change people's names to make them more powerful and better suited to his purpose. He did it to Abram and Sarai.[44] He changed it by adding the 5th letter of the Hebrew alphabet, Hei, which sounds like an 'H'. If we help change Judas which means 'betrayer', to, 'Judah'[45] which means, 'Praise the Lord', we might be able to break his power, at least for tonight.

Make sure the kids hear 'Judah'. I'll help if I can."

I have an idea. "Johnny, Give us a hand signal for chanting, Judah."

He cups his hand up and open, so it forms a J. "You'll know when the moment's right."

He starts the car, "Here they come."

We drive far enough behind them to follow, but not close enough for them to notice. I doubt Alex and Mandy would see an elephant tailing them, they are so into each other. About ten minutes later, we get to an industrial park with several low one-story buildings with rollup garage doors.

A friend of my Dads has a business here, fixing up motorcycles on the side.

Johnny asks, "Do you know where the closest hospital to here is?"

I think before answering, "Yeah, Drew to Missouri and cut over to Jeffords, it's right there."

"Good. Here are the keys for the car, just in case." I start to argue and point out that I'm fifteen, I can't drive without an adult and Johnny turns to me, "Look, these kids are unsaved, if they die; it's over for them. You need keys to drive, I don't. I might be a little tied up with Judas and you might need to get these kids to the hospital fast. Okay?"

I absorb what Johnny's saying, "Okay."

I check my cell and make sure it's on vibrate. Let's go. Vania grabs my hand as I get out, she says, "Your new name is Mal as in Malware. We're going to make Judas malfunction." I nod and let Vania and Johnny lead the way. I feel an adrenaline rush hit me like I just mainlined coffee.

Some kind of techno beat music greats us as we walk closer to the building. I can faintly make out some satanic lyrics as we get closer. Two beat up cars are blocking the doorway at the last building on the right. I smell a sweet burning smell as we get closer to the building. Some Goth kids are passing a cigarette between themselves. They're inhaling then holding their breath. One starts to cough. I've never smelled it before, but they must be smoking pot. A tall guy with chains, waves at Vania, "Who's your friend? Want a hit?" He offers us the cigarette as we pass.

Vania nods her head no and holds out her pacifier necklace signifying she's here to do X. She introduces me, "Malware this is Dodger." No one seems to notice Johnny. He must have made himself invisible.

Dodger looks Vania up and down, "Maybe we can grind later on the dance floor."

Vania smiles, "In your dreams." We walk off towards the party.

Johnny grabs Vania and me each by an elbow, nods at the bouncer and guides us into the door. The music is deafening. I'm glad we have hand signals. Johnny heads to the bar and grabs us each a Redbull.

"Don't drink it, it's just for looks," Johnny reminds us.

The lights dim even further and a disco ball shoots twinkling light everywhere. The place is getting pretty packed. I don't recognize most of the kids. Glow sticks wave back and forth in the dark. With the pounding music and the strobe lights flashing, I feel I've been transported to another world. Kids on the dance floor appear to move in stop motion from the strobe light effect. Many are grinding their hips together to the rhythm of the music. Some touching. The beat, the drugs and the alcohol are definitely lowering people's inhibitions. I watch one couple in amazement, wondering if they know what they look like. I get a quick look at their faces during the flashes of light from the strobe. I'm shocked, it's Mandy and Alex. I look away to follow Johnny and Vania. We head back further into the crowd. I'm amazed at how well I blend in; nobody gives us a second look. Vania and I keep following Johnny deeper into the party.

We pass some smaller rooms that used to be offices. We duck in looking for anyone in trouble. Kids are drinking and popping various pills. Some are licking papers with stickers on them.

Vania puts her pacifier in her mouth. I unwrap the lollipop I brought, and suck on it. We stop to talk to some people Vania knows. I nod my head, pretending to be in on the conversation, but I can't hear a thing. Vania has to bow her head and scream into the ear of the other Goth's to be heard. They do the same with her. We walk around the party, looking for Judas, doubling back to the front. I wonder briefly if he's invisible, watching us. Then I think he wouldn't want to miss out on hurting humans. So many of them are drugged out, easy pickings. We start a second circuit around the party. The music's beat gets faster and more kids gyrate on the dance floor. The lyrics are definitely more satanic. My egghead brain thinks this is how the start of ancient roman orgies must have felt. Some of the kids are drunk. They look unsteady on their feet.

The next time we get to the tiny offices we see Judas in the first one, handing out drugs for cash. We quickly pull our heads out.

Four more doorways down, Johnny motions me in. Three kids are passed out on the floor obviously in trouble. Their eyes are rolled back up into their heads and they're barely breathing. One of them is lying where he puked. Johnny makes the J signal to Vania, she nods and makes her way over to the D. J. booth. Johnny bends down and picks up two guys one in each arm, he gestures me to pick up the remaining girl. As I do I notice my cell is buzzing. I can't check my text and pick up the girl at the same time. I'm afraid to look. I'm afraid it's from Judas. He's only four doors down. If Judas catches me here, I'm afraid of what he'll do. I push that thought back and do my best to follow Johnny back through the crowd.

As I follow Johnny, carrying the girl, a guy flashes me the screen on his phone. It says, 'yell Judah'. All of a sudden, I hear Vania over the mike, louder than the music, chanting 'Judah,' 'Judah,' 'Judah.' Suddenly the place erupts with a thousand kids yelling 'Judah' over and over at the top of their lungs.

I see Judas come out of the back room. Some of the kids point him out and the crowd goes wild, like he's a rock star. They chant even louder. I can see the fury on his face. He's yelling for them to stop. Kids in the crowd just think he's being modest and keep up the chant. He pushes his way forward trying to reach Vania up on the DJ stand at the other end of the room. She gets down and heads for the exit. The chant now has a life of its own. It's ringing throughout the building. One of the Goth's steps in front of Judas, trying to speak to him, blocking Judas's way. I look back in time to see him punch the Goth with all his fury, teeth and blood go flying. I knew Judas was violent. I didn't expect to see his wrath in such a public place. Judas continues to pummel the kid with punches. Johnny finds us an exit, and runs to get the car while carrying the two kids. I follow, trying to catch up. He drives back to pick me up struggling with the girl.

Johnny yells, "Drive as fast as you can. I'm going back in for Vania."

I look down at the ignition. The car's on, but there is no key in the ignition. I stick the key in to make myself feel better. I put the car in gear and head toward the hospital with my comatose patients. All three are passed out. It's deathly quiet. The car smells like puke.

I drive as fast as I can and honk my horn as I go through a light that is turning red.

My heart is pounding as I pull up to the emergency room, I run in yelling, "Help, there are three people dying in my car! Get a gurney." Immediately, one or two nurses run out to my car along with two paramedics who had just dropped off a patient.

"What happened?" One of the nurses asked.

"They were drinking."

A thought pops into my mind, I know it's from the Holy Spirit; "Someone slipped them GHB."

"Please treat them, please hurry; there's still time to save them," I say.

The paramedics are busy hooking them up to IV's and now a mixture of nurses and doctors are working on them. I hear a couple mention the alcohol and GHB.

Another nurse comes up, "Honey what are their names?"

"I don't know, I just saw them passed out and someone helped me load them into a car, I drove as fast as I could to get here." By now, the hospital staff is rushing their patients into the hospital.

Suddenly Johnny walks up to my side and says, "Get in, I'll drive."

I'm surprised to see him. I get in the car quickly and we drive away.

"Is Vania safe?" I ask.

"Yes. I went in and got her out. I got a couple of the kids from the party to give her a ride home. After that, the cops arrived and started arresting people, for the drugs and underage drinking. The Judah chant worked. Judas's control was broken and he fled. The kids were so flustered by the cops coming in; they didn't think to arrange to move the rave elsewhere. When Judas's hands were tied spiritually by the chant, his hold on the crowd was broken."

Johnny smiles at me, "We averted a huge disaster today, 'Praise God.' "

"Are those kids going to be okay?" I ask.

"They'll survive, but there is still a battle going on for their souls until they choose God."

Johnny gets me to my house right before my ten thirty curfew.

Johnny escorts me to my front door and walks in with me. I turn to him and say, "Thank you for everything you're doing to help us."

Johnny smiles, "You're welcome."

"Do you know when this will be over?"

"When it's over," he says with another smile.

"Hey you're getting pretty good with the zingers now," I smile.

"It helps to relieve the stress."

"Yes, it does," I agree.

We walk into the living room where my Dad is watching TV.

"Awful early for a costume party, Halloween isn't for another three weeks." Dad says.

"This is my new every day look; how do you like it?"

"It's you," he says.

Johnny says, "Goodnight Mr. Laughlin."

"Goodnight Johnny."

"Johnny I know you go to church, which one do you go to?"

"I have a couple of them I go to. There are some that really need my help."

My Dad asks, "What do you do for them, help out with the kids?"

"Sometimes, mainly whatever I'm asked to do."

Of course, I know he's referring to what God asks him to do. It sure is interesting watching angels interact with humans.

Johnny says goodnight again and leaves.

My Dad turns to me and says, "Honey, are you sure Seth has nothing to worry about?"

I'm so shocked I laugh, "Dad, trust me, Johnny does not like me in that way."

My Dad gives me a look like I'm being naïve. "Honey you're a very pretty girl. A lot of guys are going to try and be friends with you hoping it develops into something more."

Arguing with my Dad is a lost cause. I can't explain to him that Johnny is an angel. I can't stop hanging around Johnny until the reason he's here is gone.

"Dad, Vania, Johnny, Carrie and I are like a Club at our school. If we can get more kids to join great. I've explained that Seth is my boyfriend and believe it or not, Johnny has a long distance relationship too. That's one reason we can be friends because both our hearts are tied up else where."

"We'll see," my Dad says.

I just roll my eyes. I can tell he still doesn't believe me. I say good-night and head toward the bathroom to take a shower. I can't wait to take all this makeup off and get the goo out of my hair. I take so long in the shower that I run out of hot water. By the time, I'm out and dressed for bed, I'm exhausted. I fall on the bed and sleep straight thru until morning. I meant to call Vania and talk to her, but in my exhaustion, I forgot.

The next day at church, I see Carrie. She comes up to me and says, "Did you hear about the rave last night?"

I truthfully answer, "No," because I hadn't heard anything about it.

"What happened?" I ask.

"Some mystery person dropped off a bunch of drugged out kids from our school at the hospital. They almost died. They're still in the hospital, but they all should live. Anyway, rumor has it the kids got sick at that big party Jude was throwing."

"Really? That's awful; I hope the kids are okay."

I wish I could tell Carrie what's really going on; but Johnny said not to. I trust his judgment because I know where it's coming from.

At least I have Vania I can confide in. Maybe Johnny's helping her find a church to go to. After last night, I forgot to ask if she wanted to come to church with us. I know her mom probably won't take her. Vania seems to be very independent out of necessity. I get the feeling she's had a rough life. I'll call her and make sure she's okay as soon as I get home from church.

When I get home, I head up to my room for privacy. I dial Vania's number. I get a disconnect signal. Now I'm worried.

"Mom can you drive me over to Vania's house; her phone isn't working."

"Honey I can't. I have to help your little brother with his science project for school."

I can't ask my Dad; he's taking his nap and insists on not being disturbed. This is awful; I can't get in touch Vania or Johnny.

I guess I'll just wait until one of them gets in touch with me.

I don't hear from either of them on Sunday, so I have to wait until lunch on Monday.

I see Jude in the hall and manage to avoid him. I can see him out of the corner of my eye staring at me. I wonder what his next step will be. If I keep ignoring him maybe, he'll just leave me alone. I wonder if he saw me at his rave or recognized me.

In my second class, of course he's my lab partner. Jude turns to me and puts his head next to mine before I can react, he says, "How did you enjoy my party, mouse?" He grabs my hand, gives it a squeeze, and won't let go.

I figure I'll nip this in the bud so I say loudly so everyone can hear, "Don't touch me!" The teacher stops talking and everyone stares at us.

Jude keeps his cool and his smile gets bigger. He says, "Sorry, we just started dating and had our first fight, it's my fault."

I look at him in amazement. He's so devious. I protest, "It's not true."

The teacher looks at me, obviously not believing me, because who would turn down the chance to date popular, handsome Jude.

She says, "Megan, please keep your personal problems out of the classroom."

When I get to the lunchroom, all the kids are buzzing about how great the party was until the cops got there. It turns out the three kids who got sick were in one of Carrie's classes and some of Vania's. I sit down; I can't wait to tell them about what Jude's trying to pull now.

Before I can open my mouth, Jude plops down next to me puts his arm around my shoulder and kisses me on the cheek in front of everyone, saying, "Hi mouse."

I go to slap him, but he was expecting it and stands up behind me out of reach. From a few tables away I see how it could look like we are playing fighting especially since he has his charming look going for him and he's obviously enjoying himself.

Vania stands up and says, "Leave her alone!"

Jude looks around at all the kids watching us and says, "It's just a lover's quarrel. Vania stop being so jealous."

Jude looks at me squeezes my shoulders, and blows me a kiss while walking away. He speaks loudly making sure he's the center of attention. "I'll see you after school, mouse, don't be mad at me for not staying for lunch; I really have to finish my paper. If only you hadn't worn me out this weekend. Love you Megan, bye baby."

Carrie looks at me and says, "Wow, you're going out with the cutest most popular guy in school. What happened to Seth?"

Vania and I speak up at the same time, "She's not," "I'm not."

"Carrie believe me, this is a twisted game he's playing. I was with Johnny and Vania most of the weekend and they know I have nothing to do with him."

Johnny and Vania both answer, "True."

Johnny says, "He's trying to prove a point about messing with him. We kind of ruined his party this weekend."

"You're the ones who called the cops," Carrie guesses.

"Sort of," Johnny says, he continues, "He's going to try and paint Vania as a jealous old girlfriend. Vania and I are going to pretend we're dating. Luckily, Seth doesn't go to school here but with the internet, we're going to have to do some damage control. Jude has played this game for eons and he's good at it."

Math class I avoid going in until the last second, my hands full of books. I barely realize Jude's hand is on my shoulder, giving the appearance that he's walking into class with me, escorting me to my seat just like any other attentive boyfriend. My situation is unbelievable. If it weren't happening to me, I wouldn't believe it. Jude lets his hand linger on the back of my chair every chance he gets. I push it off once or twice. It just makes things worse.

The next thing I know, there is someone at the door delivering flowers.

The teacher opens the door, takes the flowers and reads the card. The next thing I know she's blushing.

She hands me the flowers and the card, "You really should put this someplace private."

Jude looks up and says, "I told the florist to put the card in an envelope."

I start to protest that they're not mine; we're not dating. I feel the card tugged out of my hand and the kid next to me, Keith reads it out loud, "Megan my mouse, Thanks for making my first time so special, can't wait to see you alone this weekend, Love Jude, your lion."

\* \* \*

The damage is done. Damon/Judas/Jude has managed to ruin my reputation at this school in one planned gesture. I am so hurt by this gossip, I want to cry. By lunch tomorrow, everyone except Vania, Johnny and Carrie is going to believe I slept with Jude. During the rest of class, I'm sure he's sending me loving looks. I pray and do my best to ignore it.

When the bell rings. I go to leave. The teacher makes me carry the flowers out of the classroom. I dump them in the nearest trash can. I go to the nearest restroom rip up the card and flush it.

After school, I go up to Johnny and Vania and tell them what happened in Math class. Vania looks horrified. I can barely hold back tears. I'm afraid if I cry, Jude will show up and know that his strategy is working; of course, that will make my situation worse.

Johnny says, "He has figured out what you value most, your reputation and your values. This is where he is working hardest to destroy you. You must not look weak. Deny him calmly and laugh it off. Let Seth know what has happened, as far as the rumor. Even tell your parents. If you try to keep it hidden from people, they will be more likely to believe the rumor. If you deny and go on the offensive, it will ultimately fail. You can't worry what others are thinking. You must carry on as if nothing has happened. Gossip cannot change who you are. Only you can change who you are."

Vania looks at me and smiles, "I know who you are."

Johnny says, "So do I."

I say, "I'm still me. I know who I am and so does Seth."

Johnny also adds, "Go tell your pastor too. We'll set up a prayer group and a support system, you are not alone Megan."

When I get home, I tell my parents about the vicious rumor Jude is spreading. "Well honey we know it hurts. With in a month the kids will be listening to gossip about someone else and they'll forget. You'll see. In the meantime, you're dealing with it the right way."

"Johnny, Carrie and Vania know it's not true, too. They're starting a prayer group for me," I say.

"I have to call Seth and tell him," I continue, "and Pastor Bill, I need all the support I can get."

"Honey, we're proud of how you're handling this, we know it seems like the end of the world right now; we know it's embarrassing that so many kids are willing to believe a lie. But this really will end and in a few months, no one will remember," my Dad says, as he gives me a hug.

First, I call Pastor Bill and tell him about the lie Jude is spreading.

"Believe it or not, you are not the first girl a guy has lied and bragged about sleeping with to his friends; try your best to avoid him. Let everyone know he is lying. Eventually his character will catch up with him. People will put together all the lies he's told and see him for what he is."

"Thanks Pastor." We say a quick prayer for God to give me the strength to deal with this assault on my character.

I hang up and call Seth. He answers on the first ring.

"Hi, are you hanging around the phone waiting for me to call?" I ask.

"I'm so glad you called, your homecoming is only two weeks away and I need to know what you're going to wear."

My heart hurts from what I have to tell him, "I don't know if you're going to want to come anymore. There's this guy at school spreading a nasty lie that I slept with him." I can't help myself, I start to cry, "It's not true; I've never had anything to do with him. Carrie, Vania and Johnny know the truth; you can speak to them. I love you Seth; I'm afraid he's trying to break us apart."

"Hey Megs, don't cry, I know it's not true; I know how you are when I hold you; Of course I don't believe any stupid rumor. Of course, I'm coming to homecoming with you. When everyone sees us together, they'll see how in love we are and know he's a liar. It's okay sweetie, everything's okay," Seth says.

Seth makes me feel better. But everything is not okay. As long as Judas/Jude/Damon is here to ruin people and capture souls.

I spend the night barely sleeping. I wonder if I should transfer out of my classes. At least having Jude in some of my courses, I can keep an eye on him and stop him from doing as much damage. If I transfer out, I have no way of knowing what's going on. I am the best one to deal with Jude because I know what he is. This might be a blessing in disguise.

Maybe by sticking close to me he'll do less damage to others. Jude might be limiting his effectiveness.

At least, while I'm strategizing how I'm going to deal with Jude; I begin to feel more in control and less like a victim. I t doesn't make everything okay, but at least I can face tomorrow.

The next day I see Mandy in the hall. I walk up to her with a smile on my face. I've missed hanging out with her.

Mandy walks up to me, grabs my arm looks in a classroom, sees it's empty, takes me in and closes the door.

She turns to me with a look of anger on her face, "How dare you be all preachy to me about not sleeping with Alex and here you are sleeping with Jude. Are you doing it to be popular? That's it. You're jealous of me and my friends so your sleeping with Jude to get 'in'. You're such a hypocrite."

I look at Mandy with shock on my face. It never dawned on me that she would believe a lie like that.

"Mandy, I have not slept with Jude. I love Seth and would never cheat on him. Come on, think! You know me, I'm waiting for marriage."

Mandy looks at me puzzled. "Both Alex and Jude say you did. Why would he lie?"

"Jude is mad at me for breaking up his party the other night. Alex would love for the rumor to be true, because he wants to sleep with you. Carrie, Vania and Johnny know I didn't sleep with Jude. I was either with them or with my parents the whole weekend. They can vouch for me. I also called Seth and told him about it. He's still taking me to homecoming. Mandy, please be careful around Jude, he's dangerous."

Mandy looks at me, "I'm sorry. I should've figured this out. When I first heard I was so shocked because it didn't sound like something you would do. Don't worry. I'll let Alex know Jude is lying. Guys know guys lie about these things all the time, to seem more manly."

"Thanks Mandy. I could use your help living this rumor down," I give her a hug.

The bell rings and we both head off to our classes.

I'm starting to feel better. Yesterday, my world was one of embarrassment. Today, it's about taking my world back.

# Chapter Eight

## Friends and Frenemies

In English class, I try to forget about Jude. The teacher asks us to write a 500-word paper on any topic we like. I was going to write about being a Goth for a night; I've changed my mind. I'm writing about when a lie is spread to damage someone's reputation. I will use my own experience as an example. I hope we get asked to read them out loud.

In science class, we are going to be dissecting a frog. The frogs arrive already soaked in formaldehyde. The sickly sweet smell fills the classroom quickly. One of the students is assigned to hand out lab coats and gloves. The teacher hands out the frogs; Jude and I get our frog.

I ask him, "Would you like to do the dissecting?"

"Absolutely, I love cutting things up."

For once, I believe he's telling the truth. I take up my notebook and start identifying the internal organs. I stand as far away from him as I can. I'm afraid he might cut me with the scalpel if he gets a chance.

"You can stand closer; I won't bite," Jude says as he smiles.

"No thank you." I don't believe him for a minute. I know how dangerous he is.

I manage to keep my attention on the job at hand. Jude tries to get me to mislabel a couple of the organs. I pretend he's not even here and just take my notes. I'm thankful for when the bell rings. Two more classes and the day is done. Today tickets for the homecoming game and dance go on sale so most of the buzz is about who's going with whom. Several girls I barely know ask if I'm going with Jude. I take the time to explain he's mad at me about breaking up his party and that I never slept with him. I also let them know I'm going with my boyfriend Seth.

They all seem happy that they might have a chance with Jude. I just shake my head amazed that they don't seem to be fazed about his lying.

I have to remember, life isn't always fair. Sometimes those who are idolized get a free pass on bad behavior. At least in this life.

When I run into Vania at lunch I ask, "Did you get a new phone number? I tried to call you on Sunday and they said the number was disconnected."

"No. Sometimes my Mom forgets to pay the bill." I wonder if Vania's mom is having money problems. I keep it to myself and change the subject.

"Are you guys going to the game and dance?" I ask Vania and Johnny.

Johnny answers, "Yes, of course. We'll be on the look out for more of Jude's games."

Carrie looks up from her salad, "Boy you guys are quite the crime fighting duo."

Carrie still doesn't know Johnny's an angel.

Johnny looks at her, "I basically live for that kind of stuff."

Carrie answers honestly, "You'll probably go into law enforcement when you graduate."

Johnny just nods his head in agreement.

I change the subject, "Carrie, I spoke to Seth last night and they're all set to drive down next weekend. Pastor Bill has agreed to put them both up at his house."

"I know, I can't wait. Maybe we can get Robby to set Jude straight," Carrie says.

"Let's try and keep them apart, I don't want to cause a scene. You know how Robby is, it wouldn't take much to set him off."

Vania looks at me, "How are you surviving the rumor mill?"

"I can't believe how many girls want to go out with Jude, even with the lies he's been spreading about me. Aren't they afraid the same thing would happen to them, or even worse?" I answer.

"I only have one more class to suffer through today with him. It hasn't been as bad as it could be." With homecoming preparations under-way, people are more concerned with their own social life than mine.

As we're leaving the cafeteria, I hear my name paged, "Megan Laughlin to the front office, Megan Laughlin to the front office."

Several people tease me on my way to the front office, "Oh, you're in trouble now." "Uh, Oh" "What'd you do?"

I get there and Mrs. Wilcox, one of the counselors invites me into her office.

"Have a seat, Megan."

She gestures to one of two chairs in front of her desk. Mrs. Wilcox closes the door and sits behind her desk. The office is so small, it feels claustrophobic.

"How do you know Samuel Donner?"

"Samuel Donner?" I say. "I don't know him." I've never heard the name before.

"He specifically asked to speak to you," she looks at me and folds her hands. It's like she's expecting me to reveal something.

"I don't know anyone named Sam Donner," now I'm puzzled.

I have no clue what this conversation is about or where it's going.

"Should I know Samuel Donner?" I ask Mrs. Wilcox.

She sighs and sits back in her chair, "He said he didn't know you. In twenty years of counseling I've never run into anything like this before."

Mrs. Wilcox leans forward onto her desk and says, "This is going to sound a little crazy. But he says he saw you in a dream and he needs to speak to you. Alone."

"Okay. I still have no idea who Sam Donner is. If you want to bring him in, I'll speak to him," I say.

"That won't be possible. Sam is still in the ICU at the hospital. He woke up out of a three day coma this morning. He was one of three kids dropped off at the hospital unconscious after suffering from an overdose at a party Saturday night. He woke up asking to speak to you. Sam said it was a matter of life or death," Mrs. Wilcox continues, "I called your parents and spoke to the principal. Because of the unusual circumstances of the case, they have given me permission to take you to speak to him. If it's okay with you. Do you have any idea what this is about?"

"I'm not sure," I answer truthfully, "But I'm willing to find out."

Mrs. Wilcox and I walk out to her car. We get in and drive most of the way in silence.

"I've heard of things like this happening before, but thought they were made up or exaggerated. So you've never met him before?" She asks, then adds, "He does go to school here."

"No. I haven't. I have no idea why he would dream about me or how I could possibly help him."

Mrs. Wilcox pulls in the lot a few minutes later. We walk up to the volunteer at the front desk who directs us up to the second floor.

We get off the elevator in the ICU; Mrs. Wilcox takes a seat to wait for me while a nurse takes me back to Sam's room.

I walk in and he appears to be sleeping, the nurse says softly, "Sam you have a visitor." She looks at me, "I'll close the door to give the two of you some privacy. Just hit the buzzer on his bed if you need anything."

"Thank you."

When I look back at Sam, he's watching me. He looks terrible. His lips are chapped and dried out. There's almost no color in his face. We got those kids out so fast Saturday night that I had no chance to look at them. I couldn't have picked his face out of a line up.

"You look exactly the same as in my dream. You're even wearing the same clothes I described to the nurse." Sam's voice is raspy, like it's hard for him to talk.

"I don't know you," I say stating the obvious.

"I know," he tries to chuckle, "Can you hold up the water cup so I can have a drink?"

He takes a sip and just watches me. "Are you an angel?" Sam asks.

"No," I pause trying to think of something to say, "I go to your school."

"I need to tell you what I saw, in my dream. Saturday night when I got to the party with Bebe and Vaughn, I only had one coke. They're telling me someone slipped me that GHB in my drink, enough to kill. It's weird. Why would someone want to kill me?"

Sam pauses to take a sip of water, "My throat is killing me," he says.

I don't think he caught the irony of what he just said.

"Anyway, some time after I came to the hospital; I died. It wasn't beautiful like people say. I didn't see a white light," Sam shudders. "It was dark and I was lost. Someone kept whispering, 'you're dead, you're mine,' over and over. I kept walking to get away from the voice, until I fell into this dark tunnel. It led into a ring of fire and coming up to me; I could see this lake of fire. I held my hands out trying to push myself away and that's when I got this."

He holds up his hands, the palms are all blistered from a bad burn.

He continues, "I didn't have these burns when they admitted me. They happened after I died on the table. The doctors brought me back. It really freaked them out. They say I had a reaction to the medication, but I know the truth. When I died, I went to hell."

Sam pauses and shudders again.

"They must have started my heart one second before I fell into that lake of fire. One more second and I would be in hell," Sam is losing his voice; I give him another sip of water.

"After they started my heart, I had a dream. I could feel my palms burning; I know how close I came. I called out to God to save me, please save me."

"That's when I saw you. Dressed in the same clothes you're wearing right now. You said, 'I know how you can be saved.' "

"Please tell me how."

I sit in shock for a minute, "Of course."

"Do you know Jesus?"

"Yes. I was christened when I was a baby. I should be saved. I thought I was saved. My parents and my pastor always told me I was saved. I go to church sometimes. I'm a good person. Why did this happen to me?" Sam starts to cry.

I nod my head, "I'm sorry Sam. Its more than going to church and being a good person."

"You have to repent of your sins. For all have sinned[46], including me Sam. Repent means to turn away."

"Repent doesn't mean to say 'sorry' and then keep doing the same wrong. You also have to ask for forgiveness[47]. Jesus died on the cross for you. His innocent blood was shed for you. The wages of sin are death.[48]

Next, after you repent and ask forgiveness, you need to ask Jesus to come live in your heart. Jesus rose again from the dead and he offers us the gift of eternal life.[49] You have to consciously choose him, choose to love him and follow him.

When you have done these things you will truly be saved."[50]

"Sam, you can be saved right now."

"Okay, I'll pray out loud, if I do it wrong you'll tell me?" Sam looks hopeful.

"Sure."

Sam takes a deep breathe and says, "Repent. That's first." I nod my head.

"Dear Lord in heaven, thank you for my second chance, I promise to do my best to stop doing wrong things. Dear Jesus I'm sorry you had to die on the cross for my sins, please forgive me. Please come into my heart. I choose to love you of my own free will. Thank you."

Sam looks up, "was that okay?"

I smile, "That was perfect. There are angels in heaven rejoicing right now for you."[51]

Sam says again, "Are you sure you're not an angel?"

I laugh, "No, just a saved sinner. Like you."

Sam smiles, "Like me."

He gets a serious look on his face, "I have to tell my Mom and Dad. They think they're saved, maybe they're not."

"Where are they?" I ask.

"They've been praying for me for the last three days along with my pastor. When I woke up this morning they left to go home and take care of a few things."

"Well it looks like their prayers worked. Did you tell them about me?"

"No," Sam answers sheepishly, "I didn't want them to think I was crazy."

"I understand. I wouldn't have told anyone either." Of course, I have a secret of my own that only Vania knows.

Sam looks at me, his face is troubled again.

"There's something I saw, when I was falling to the lake of fire. I don't know if you can help or if you should know for your own safety."

"What is it Sam?" My stomach is suddenly tied in knots.

"Jude was down there waiting to greet me. The flames weren't hurting him. He wasn't alone. Jude was laughing and he had his arm around my buddy."

"Who? Sam? Who?"

"Brody. My friend Brody, he was at the party with me." Sam looks like he's going to cry.

"Hold on Sam let me check with the nurse. Maybe he's alive. Maybe it's not too late."

I walk out to the nurse's station.

"Hi. I was just visiting with Samuel Donner?"

"Oh yes," the nurse says.

"He's very worried about his friend Brody; is he still alive?"

"You can tell him Brody is fine; he's scheduled to be released some time this afternoon."

"Thank you." I'm relieved; there still might be a chance to save him.

I walk down the hall sticking my head in the doorways, looking for Brody.

I find him three doors down. When I stick my head in, I see a grayness hovering over Brody. I walk in and say, "Hi Brody."

He opens his eyes to look at me. I say, "Sam is really worried about you." Brody looks at me coldly.

"I think I can help you," I say.

"Get out." "You can't help me. Get out!" He screams. I leave just as a nurse enters to check on Brody. I go back into Sam's room. I sit back down.

"Brody's still alive," I try to look hopeful, "There might be a chance to save him."

Sam shakes his head sadly, "I don't think so, he was already in hell, I don't know but I get the feeling he made a deal with the devil."

"Sam, Jude is bad news stay away from him. I'll try to find out more about Brody to see if it's too late for him. I honestly don't know."

I get out my cell and take a pencil and paper off the table next to him.

"Here's my number, and Pastor Bill's phone number, from my church.

Is it okay if I have him drop into see you? He'd be a good one to talk to about Brody."

"What about you other friend? The girl?"

"I don't know her name; we just met her at the club that night."

"She wasn't in your vision though?"

"It wasn't a vision, it really happened," Sam holds up his palms to show me again. "It's real. Hell is a real place. We do go somewhere when we die. And I'm never going to hell again."

"You're right, you're saved. Now you can help the rest of us save others."

Sam looks very tired. I decide it's time to go.

"Sam if you need me for anything, I'm just a phone call away. You look like you need to rest."

Sam looks up, "Thank you. I'm not afraid to sleep now. Maybe I'll see you in school," he puts his head on the pillow and closes his eyes.

I walk back to the lobby where Mrs. Wilcox is waiting.

"Is he okay?" She asks.

"Yes. He's fine."

We walk in silence to the car.

I can tell Mrs. Wilcox has some questions she wants to ask.

When we get buckled in the car, she turns to me and says, "You know he described what you're wearing today. He had a dream; you were in it."

"I know."

"When he woke out of the coma, he insisted on speaking to you. The nurses said he was too upset to sleep. That's why I brought you to speak to him. Are you okay? Is there anything you want to tell me?"

I say, "I don't know if you're a Christian or not, but Sam went to hell. That's why his hands are burned. Hell's a real place. Sam wanted be saved. That's why he wanted to speak to me."

I look at Mrs. Wilcox. I can tell she looks uncomfortable.

I told her the truth. That's all I can do. The rest is between her and God.

We finish the rest of the ride back to school in silence.

The rest of the week flies by quickly. Brody and Sam aren't back in school yet; so there is not much I can do to save Brody. I keep my distance from Jude/Damon the best I can. One day as lab partners, he manages to nick me with a scalpel. I tell the teacher, Jude did it on purpose, but he acts so sorry; she doesn't believe me.

I can tell Jude/ Damon is up to something. In Math class, he still pretends we're a couple. I ignore him as much as possible. In English class, the teacher pulls me aside after I turn in my paper about gossip, and tells me they'll have a counselor speak to Jude about what he did. She does not let me read my paper out loud to the class, because it's 'he said/ she said' and she doesn't want to get involved. I've done all the damage control I can.

Friday morning in Microbiology class, Jude seems giddy with happiness. He has to be planning something for this weekend. I meet Johnny, Vania and Carrie in the lunchroom.

I ask, "Jude is planning something for this weekend, what should we do?"

Vania snaps at me, "Is that all you care about? Does every discussion have to be about him? What about us? We have lives too."

"I'm sorry, Vania."

She looks at me, "I'm sorry, I didn't mean to snap."

"I'm under a lot of stress right now."

I look at Vania and notice she is thinner and paler than usual. I shove my sandwich and chips at her, "Here please eat this, I lost my appetite and I hate to throw it away."

Vania looks at me, "Are you sure?" She starts to dig in.

"Yes. If you had classes with Jude, you'd lose your appetite too."

I'm wondering, Vania's phone is disconnected, her clothes are old, and maybe she and her mom are having money problems. Vania doesn't look like she's getting enough to eat. I decide I'm going to start packing my lunches and make sure I have enough for Vania too.

That day after school, I wait for Vania and Johnny at the auditorium bench where my parents pick me up.

Johnny arrives first, "You're right, Jude is planning something. I'm going to work hard at preventing it. I don't think you can help on this one, just pray. Take care of Vania this weekend if you can, I won't be available."

With that, he takes off. Vania shows up a minute later, "you just missed Johnny," I say. "Would you come to my house for dinner tonight, it would be nice to have someone to talk to."

"Don't you have to ask your parents first?"

"Nah. They love you. You add some excitement to our lives."

"Okay. Thanks. I get a little lonely at home. We had to cancel our cable TV. And we're behind on the phone. Money's tight right now. My Mom's working all she can, but her car broke down and she had to pay to get it fixed. Then her tooth got a cavity, which became infected, so she had to take care of that. Things will get better. They always do."

The way Vania says it, makes me think she doesn't believe things are going to get better any time soon.

"Well then, let's call your Mom at work and see if you can spend the night."

She smiles at me, "That would be great."

We stay up Friday night and watch three of the 'Left Behind' movies in a row. I can't believe she hasn't seen them before. We watch the rapture scene twice. It's just too cool. About midnight, I get a call on my cell I reach for it and answer, because it says "Seth."

It's not Seth; I hit the speakerphone button so Vania can hear.

"Hello mouse, hello Sly-van-ia. Sylvania do you miss me, we had such fun. Tie score again, mouse, 2 to 2, 2 to 2, 2 to 2. Who's next? Hmmm. Who's not saved? Here's a riddle, who does mouse love the most, send to hell and let her roast? Burn her up, just like toast? Hmmm. Sleep tight. Don't let the bed bugs bite."

Somebody has died and gone to hell. My heart sinks. I'm sure it's someone I know or some one from school. Vania and I have a hard time getting to sleep. We pray for God to give us peace.

Saturday morning, Vania and I get up late. We pour big bowls of cereal and go to watch TV in the family room while we eat.

As we're watching, the news comes on, "In a tragic twist of fate, one of the teens involved in a drug overdose last weekend, was tragically killed in a car accident Friday night. Brody Gibbens, 17, a senior at Countryside High, was just released from the hospital Thursday afternoon. Brody, who was celebrating his first day at home since being released from the hospital, was driving the car, accompanied by two friends, Jewel Ferguson, 15, and Damon Lawless, 16. Jewel is in the hospital with severe but non-life threatening injuries. Damon Lawless, the only one in the car wearing a seatbelt; walked away with out a scratch. This is the second tragic death to hit Countryside High School this year. Jordan Jamisen tragically died of an apparent suicide, just 6 weeks ago. A memorial service will be held on Wednesday afternoon." I turn the TV off.

Somehow, Damon/Jude/Judas caused this crash. Vania and I just look at each other. We need to find away to stop Jude, but how?

On Monday, the mood is somber. Some of the kids are wearing black armbands in memory of Brody. Kids are car-pooling to the crash site to leave flowers, notes and stuffed animals. It seems like the whole school is going to attend the memorial service on Wednesday at a church near the high school. Damon/Jude is in school soaking up all they sympathy. It's hard for Vania, Johnny and me to watch. We know he had something to do with the crash.

The four of us head to the memorial service on Wednesday; I wish I could've done something to help Brody, but he had already made his decision before I had met him. Johnny and I watch Jude at the memorial service. The best we can do is figure out who his next target might be.

Someone unsaved, someone in turmoil, someone I know, those are the only clues we have.

By Thursday, most of the kids are now wrapped up in last minute preparations for homecoming. Carrie and I are counting down the days until we can see Seth and Robby. Their school homecoming is the same Saturday as ours so we won't get to go to both after all. Pastor Bill and his wife are graciously letting Robby and Seth camp out in their guest room for the weekend.

Friday night, once the guys have arrived, everyone is coming to our house for a late night dinner of grilled burgers. I invite Vania and her mom and Johnny too. Saturday morning we're going to hit the beach and then go to the homecoming game and dance that evening. Sunday, Robby and Seth will come to church with Pastor Bill, we'll all have lunch at Carrie's house and then Robby and Seth will drive back home.

Friday after school, I get a call from Mandy.

"Hey I miss you, Megan."

"Mandy, how have you been?"

"Oh, great everything's going great," Mandy sounds a little sad.

"Why don't you and Alex come by tonight? Seth and Robby will be here by seven. Johnny and Vania from school will be here too. We're going to grill some burgers it'll be fun."

"I'd love to, but I'm just getting over a cold. I don't want to get anybody sick. I'll see you at homecoming tomorrow. I'm just going to take it easy till then." Mandy does sound a little stuffed up.

"Okay, I'll see you at the game. Mandy, I love you. You don't have to do anything you don't want to."

"I know. I'll see you tomorrow. Bye."

Carrie, Johnny, and Vania arrive an hour later with Carrie's parents, and Vania's mom in tow. I told Mom and Dad, Johnny doesn't have any parents. They're very careful about not making him feel left out. When Vania's Mom, Cindy, finds out we all go to the same church, she says she might come when she has a day off, especially now that she knows us. When Seth and Robby arrive, I'm in heaven. I run outside when I hear a honking horn (Robby of course). Seth gets out and I give him a big hug. He feels so good I almost cry. I've missed him so much. He looks so happy, "Megs, it's okay. Hey, don't cry. I'm here and we have the whole weekend together." Pastor Bill and his wife Gina walk around to the back to give Seth and me a moment of privacy. When we walk back to the pool area, we're just in time to see Robby pick Carrie up and throw her in the pool. He then cannon balls in to rescue her with a Tarzan yell.

Pastor Bill calls out, "Let the party begin."

As we're all sitting down to eat the doorbell rings. My Dad gets up to answer it. I wish he hadn't.

Dad comes back with a big smile on his face, laughing at a joke told by Jude/Damon. I can't believe my eyes. I had told my parents about Jude.

I just about choke on my burger. Why would they let him in?

My Dad says, "I guess most of you know Damon." I forgot to tell my parents that Jude also calls himself Damon.

"Hi, Megan, Vania, Johnny. Sorry I'm late. I had a few things to set up before tomorrow."

Damon walks right up to Seth, "Who's this, my competition?" Damon sounds like he's joking. He holds out his hand for Seth to shake, "Hi, I'm Damon, Megan's lab partner, and you're . . ."

Seth stands up, wipes his hand off on napkin, and reaches out to shake Damon's hand, "I'm Seth, Megan's boyfriend."

Damon squeezes Seth's hand hard. I can see a look of shock on Seth's face. He can see now that Damon is not here for a friendly visit.

"I'm surprised you're here, I didn't invite you," I pipe up.

"Megan!" My Dad says, "That's not how we treat guests."

"How 'bout a burger, Damon?" My Dad offers.

"Sure Mr. Laughlin I'm starving," Damon smiles and takes a seat at the table.

Damon starts filling up his plate. I reach under the table and grab Seth's hand. Vania's gone pale and stopped eating. Johnny eats slowly keeping his eyes on Damon. Robby is cluelessly stuffing his face and making plays for Carrie's attention. The adults are seated at a separate table inside the porch area; we can hear them chatting away. After getting Damon a burger, my Dad rejoins them.

"Why are you here?" I ask.

Damon talks with his mouth full. "I told you, mouse. I'm here to size up the competition. Frankly, facing you all doesn't seem like much of a challenge."

Seth looks at me, "What is he talking about?"

Damon says, "Ah keeping secrets, how many of these fools don't even know what there up against?"

Robby looks up having caught the tail end of what Damon was saying.

He stands up looking down at Damon, "Is there a problem here? May be you should leave."

Damon stands up, looks Robby in the eye and says, "I'll decide when it's time to leave." He places a finger on Robby's chest and Robby goes flying a good ten feet, backwards into the pool.

Seth stands up and says, "What the . . . what's going on here?"

Johnny reaches for Damon's arm, grabs it and says, "It's time to leave. You've had your fun and games."

Johnny escorts Damon out the door while we help Robby out of the pool.

The adults think the guys were horsing around so they didn't pay any attention. They go into the house back to the front living room for coffee and desert.

Robby says as he climbs out of the pool, "What just happened isn't possible. Tell me I didn't just fly backward from a finger push. What is going on?"

Seth answers, "This is creepy, I have no idea what's happening."

Carrie looks like she's about to have a panic attack; she looks at me and says, "He said we were the competition and called us fools. He said it to Meg; She's got to know what's going on." I look around at my friends, how do I tell them? I look to Vania for help, maybe she can help me explain.

Vania says, "Tell them, they have to know; Jude is targeting them too." All eyes swivel back to me. I see Johnny opening the porch door, walking back to us; I breathe a sigh of relief. He can help me explain.

I say, "Here let Johnny explain."

As Johnny gets back, he says, "I think it's time everyone here knows. I think it's fair to say Damon is going to target everyone here. Who knows what we will be facing this weekend."

As Johnny finishes his last statement, he begins to glow brightly then levitates in case there is doubt in anyone's mind. Seth says, "What are you?" Robby for once is speechless. Carrie has a look of wonderment on her face.

Before he can be questioned, Johnny says, "I'm an angel, sent from God.[52] You know there is a spiritual war that started in heaven and is now continuing here on earth. Megan here can see angels and spirits. Because of her gift, she has attracted this evil angel who goes by many names.[53] I'm here to help bind him, but I need your help. You are saved. Your souls are safe. But many kids this weekend could be swayed by Damon to make choices that can cost them their lives and their souls. Damon can't hurt you without God's permission. God could grant him that permission; but your souls are saved. Your names are written in the book of life. We should get some sleep. You're going to need your energy for tomorrow."

Robby looks at Johnny, "This is too cool. Yeah, we can fight him for God. Hey, can we get some special weapons or like some powers? Maybe you can help us fly or something. Bring it on, oh yeah."

Johnny just shakes his head, "I'll answer everyone's questions tomorrow. Right now I've got to go back out and keep an eye on our friend. He's always up to more mischief at night when people are drinking and doing drugs; it's easier pickings for him."

As I walk Seth out to the van, before anyone else comes out, we see Damon across the street. He flashes us a peace sign then disappears.

I look at Seth, "I'm sorry I didn't tell you sooner. I just didn't know how to say, 'oh by the way, I see angels'. I didn't want you to think I was a nutcase; and I wanted to keep you safe."

Seth takes my hands, "Well Megs, tonight has been full of surprises. You see angels, huh? None of this changes the way I feel about you. I would give my life if it meant saving you. I'm glad your not alone when I'm not around. I'm glad Johnny's here to help protect you. How long have you known?"

"Only since summer camp," I answer. I start to cry. Seth and the rest are in danger and it's my fault.

Seth takes me in his arms, "It's okay, we have God on our side."

Robby comes out with Carrie, "I talked to Johnny and Vania, tomorrow at the beach we'll come up with a strategy on how to deal with Damon. Let's try to get some sleep and pray on it. Johnny's going to pick us up at eight thirty, sharp."

Everyone leaves. I help Mom clean up and then drop in the sack. I pray about what I should do, but I don't get an answer.

Ugh, my alarm goes off. It's a struggle to get out of bed. I go to the kitchen and fill a cup of coffee; then I take a quick shower, get dressed, slather on the sunscreen, pack a bag and go downstairs to sit by the front window, waiting for Johnny to pull up.

As I'm waiting, Max comes down the stairs.

"Hey Maxie," I say.

He walks up to me rubbing his eyes, he looks sad.

"What's wrong big guy?" I ask as I lift him up onto my lap for a hug.

"I had a bad dream."

"You did? What was it about?"

"This monster came into my room he said he was going to hurt you and then come for me."

A chill hits my heart. I hug Max and tell him, "It's okay Maxie, it's only a dream; Jesus will protect you. Tonight, before you go to sleep, you ask Jesus to send his angels to keep us safe and I will too. I love you Maxie."

"I love you sissy."

Johnny pulls up; I put Max down. "Go watch some cartoons. I'll see you later."

I wonder if it was a dream or if Damon came by to torment my little brother. I'll never look at bad dreams the same way again.

It's such a beautiful day at the beach; again, it's hard to believe we're in a battle for people's souls. Carrie and Robby head for the water as soon as we lay are blankets down. I'm interested to see what Vania wears to the beach. Wouldn't you know she managed to find a black suit with a lot of metal rings on it. She's also wearing a big black straw hat, black sunglasses, flip-flops and lipstick. Her hair today is a bright yellow. She actually looks quite chic.

Seth lays down a big blanket that we anchor with bags and sandals, from the wind. Seth asks Johnny, "So do you get to pick what you look like in earthly form?"

Johnny looks at Seth, "No more than you do." Seth nods his head like that makes perfect sense.

"So what did Jesus look like when he was on earth?"

"At what time on earth? He looks like whatever he wanted to look like. He is the great I AM. Does it matter to your salvation what he looks like?"

I give Seth a look, He says, "I'm curious, I might not get an opportunity like this again."

I'm surprised he's at ease with hanging out with an angel.

"Wanna arm wrestle?"

"Now you're sounding like Robby," I say.

Johnny answers, "No, I'd win, what's the point?"

Vania says, "My boyfriend can beat up your boyfriend."

We all laugh and settle back to enjoy the day, while we can.

Robby and Carrie come out of the surf and lay down to let the sun bake them dry.

Robby asks, "Dude, what's heaven like?"

Johnny appears to be thinking about his answer.

"Better. Different. It's like comparing this beach to your perfect dream beach. It would be better and different."

Robby tries another question, "What's the food like?"

Johnny answers, "Better, different."

Johnny sees he has all of our attention.

"It's hard to limit heavenly things to this world which is based in time and limited to so many physical laws. Your languages are a barrier to heavenly meanings. Your human brains are like a fly's brain compared to God. You try to fit him into a box shaped by time and space. God is bigger, different from that. His creation, this universe cannot contain him.

He is the 'I AM'.[54] Think bigger." We need time to digest everything Johnny has just said. Johnny continues, "Since we are bound by time, we need to think about what to do tonight, about Damon/Jude/Judas at the game. We need to keep an eye on him. We can eaves drop on him and those he talks to. Follow him at every opportunity. Keep praying continually the whole evening while going about the game and the dance. We can't prevent him from every evil thing he does but we can stop some. Since we have three groups we should always aim to keep him in the center of a triangle formed by us. If I ask you to do something, no matter how silly it seems, please just do it. Later, you will see why it was helpful."

I bring up something that has been haunting me, "Johnny, the other night when Brody died, Jude called. He did this awful poem, about a 'her that I love the most'. The only 'hers' that I can think of are saved, except one.

My best friend for years has been Mandy. I don't think she's saved. I'm worried he might target Mandy tonight."

"He could. But Jude's father is the father of lies. Jude could have said that to throw us off track. Tonight keep your eyes and ears alert. Signal me if anything nags at you, it could be important. If you need to speak to me, signal me to come over and have your partner cross to be with Vania. Don't drink a lot of fluids, so we can limit bathroom breaks. Have your phones ready to receive texts. Sign an x after every text; so we know it's not a fake sent by Jude. Any questions?"

Robby raises his hand and we all groan.

"I mean about tonight's plan," Johnny adds.

Robby's hand goes down. We nervously chuckle. The rest of the afternoon, we enjoy hanging out and acting our age. The afternoon passes quickly and soon it's time to head home and change for the game and then the dance. I hope this evening has as good an ending as the rave did; but I know Jude/Judas/Damon is prepared for us. He has some tricks up his sleeve. I don't think he would be so cocky if he wasn't sure; whatever the surprise is, we won't see it coming.

# Chapter Nine

## Homecoming

By the time we get to the game, Mandy and Alex are already down on the field. Both Mandy and Alex are on the homecoming court. I'm so proud of Mandy. She talks to everyone and passes out lots of hugs. She looks beautiful in a full-length iridescent cornflower blue dress. It's almost a roman toga style with one wide shoulder strap. The skirt has a waterfall effect falling in layers on the left side with a modest slit starting just above the knee. They take a ride around the field in a convertible car.

If I get a chance, I'll try to warn her about Jude. Jude is down on the field too. One of the kids who made the court had to step down due to illness and Jude is his replacement. I notice him talking quite a bit to Alex.

At one point I see him gesture towards Mandy making a crude hand sign while Alex nods his head and chuckles. I'm sure Jude is pressuring Alex to make an advance on Mandy tonight. I say a prayer for Mandy's safety.

Alex goes back to suit up for the game.

The game starts without incident. Seth and I hold each other's hand and sneak in a few hugs. We really don't see much of the game. We're as close to the field as we can get. Jude is bouncing around talking to several people, being his usual charming public self. If I didn't see his darkness shining through, I might be fooled myself. As Jude leaves a group of kids' a fight breaks out. Punches are flying. One girl gets knocked over and scratched up. A few adult parents and teachers head over to stop it. I'm sure he said something to instigate the fight. Jude is just warming up.

I am so grateful I am not alone in facing Jude. For a minute, I wonder where Zadok is and how he is doing. I wonder if he is back in heaven or somewhere here on this earth. I miss him. I wonder if in heaven we will have friendships with angels.

After the game, we get to our cars, which we parked near the exit in sight of Jude's car. We follow him to the dance.

At the dance, it's hard to enjoy ourselves. I tell Seth what happened at the Rave so he's prepared. Damon circles talking to his numerous fans. He waves to us a few times. Jude's obviously aware we are following him.

Mandy and Alex head over to talk to Seth and me. "Hi Mandy, you look beautiful," I say as I hug her.

"You too," she responds.

"Mandy and Alex this is Seth, my boyfriend."

"Nice to meet you," Alex says, holding out his hand for Seth to shake.

Alex looks at me, "Jude must be upset; he has quite the crush on you."

Seth and I look at each other, I answer, "If you only knew . . . Seth knows all about the problems I'm having with Jude." Seth nods his head, "He's deluded himself about his importance in Meg's life. We're trying to straighten him out." Seth gives me a hug of reassurance and kisses me on my head.

"He's a nice guy, I'm sure he'll come around. There are only about a dozen girls who have a crush on him," Alex says.

"Is he throwing a party after the dance?" I try to sound casual.

Alex looks at Mandy, "I don't know. If he does, we won't be attending, we have some special plans of our own. I got us a room at the Hyatt."

He winks at Seth. I look at Mandy with concern, but she's too busy looking at Alex adoringly.

We excuse our selves; Seth and I walk off to get a drink after that. Mandy is making a huge mistake and there is nothing I can do to stop it. It won't do any good to go to their parents. They're the ones that gave Alex the condoms and Mandy the pill. I wonder if their parents really realize what they've done by rolling the dice. If it comes up pregnancy or STD, will they feel okay with it?

Jude starts dancing with some of the girls who have been following him around the dance floor. One girl walks off in tears. I wonder how he insulted her. Jude is so good at it. The next girl he dances with, he has his hands on her in front of every one, she looks a little uncomfortable but doesn't stop dancing with him. One of the adult chaperones walks over and says something to him. He tones it down. I dance a slow dance with Seth; he turns me so he's watching Jude. I look over his shoulder and see Mandy and Alex leaving the dance. I feel Seth's body stiffen, I whisper in his ear, "what's he doing?"

"He just slipped something in that girl's drink." Seth takes my hand and we walk over. He bumps into her hard enough to distract her and uses his hand to knock the drink onto the floor.

"Hey!" The girl says.

"Sorry, I wasn't looking," Then Seth whispers into her ear, "Jude slipped something into your drink, be careful." Seth and I don't care if we're being obvious to Jude. We want him to know, we're not afraid of him, cautious, but not fearful. He's toying with us while searching out those he can harm.

My romantic evening with Seth has turned into a night of babysitting the dance room.

Jude comes right up to Seth and me and says, "You're so clueless, this isn't where the action is this evening. All I did was give the ball a push and now it's rolling down the hill into traffic. You can't stop it." He does a little victory dance. "Relax have some fun. Seth, Megan's hot. You know you want to. What are you waiting for man? You know you're going to marry her some day. Why wait? You're gonna miss out on years of loving her for what? You really think God cares? You think he's going to waste his time with you? You're a fool."

I hold Seth back. I can tell he wants to punch him. "Seth, he's defeated, he knows it. Jude's just a sore loser leave him alone." I drag Seth out of Jude's range.

I motion to Johnny and he sends Vania in our direction. I ask Seth, "Dance with Vania, I'll be right back." I walk over to Johnny.

"Jude says the action isn't happening here, but somewhere else. I believe him. He looks too happy."

Johnny nods his head, "He could have any number of things in the works. We angels can only be in one place at one time, so unless we know what's going down, it's still best to keep him insight, even if it turns out to be a waste of our time."

The rest of the evening passes without incident and we all feel worn out by the time the dance breaks up. We follow Jude out to his car. He leaves alone. Johnny asks, "Can you give Vania a ride home so I can follow Jude the rest of the evening?" "Sure," Seth says. We head home tired and relieved. We drop Vania off first, then me. Carrie's house is on the way to Pastor Bill's.

Seth gives me a quick hug and kiss at the door. We don't want to tempt our passion into taking over. Jude was right. We want to. But God is more right. And to please him, we wait.

Sunday morning, I get up an hour before church, so I have time for a cup of coffee and to put on some makeup. I have dark circles under my eyes from lack of sleep. I want Seth to see me at my best. I put on a cute summer dress, since we're going to lunch at Carrie's right after church. I bring my swimsuit just in case.

On the morning news, they mention there was a break in at a near by high school. Computers were stolen out of the computer lab. I wonder if Jude had anything to do with that.

When Max comes down stairs I ask him, "How were your dreams last night?"

"Better. I did what you said. I asked Jesus to give me good dreams and to have his angels guard me while I sleep."

I give him a hug, "Good guy, I love you."

"Yeah, do we have any eggo's left?" He squirms out of my arms and into the kitchen. We head out the door shortly after Max finishes his breakfast.

At church, Seth and Robby are already there, having come early with Pastor Bill and Gina. Seth has his car packed up, ready to head home after lunch at Carrie's. Seth and I sit next to each other during church. Ironically, Pastor Bill's sermon is on the servant attitude of angels and what we can learn from their example.

After church, and plenty of good bys, we head over to Carrie's house. Seth and I are alone in his car since Robby hitched a ride with Carrie and her parents.

"I'm sorry this weekend didn't turn out like we planned," I say. I'm disappointed that we didn't have as much romance as I would have liked.

"Are you kidding? This was one of the best weekends of my life. I got to be around you and God gave me, us, confirmation that there is a whole spiritual world going on around us. I have an angel as a friend and we're serving God together. What could be better?"

"But what about Jude? He's going to be out to get us!"

"So? Haven't evil angels always been out to get us? We have God's protection. Don't worry so much."

I'm amazed at Seth's point of view. I can't believe how nonchalant he is about the good/bad angel thing.

When we get to Carrie's house, she's drying off from Robby having thrown her in the pool. I look at her and shake my head and say, "again?"

"Don't worry, I've set limits, only once a party and never on a major Holiday like Easter or Christmas."

"We'll that should work."

"And if I'm wearing my cell phone and he ruin's it, I get a free up-grade. I think I'll have a top of the line one by Christmas," Carrie looks ecstatic. Robby would drive me nuts after one day, but she's obviously in heaven.

Robby enters the patio from the house and says, "Surprise, guess who's here."

I turn around expecting, Johnny and Vania. "Hi everyone, hi mouse, mind getting me a coke, Robby, my man?" Of course, it's Jude.

"Help yourself, on the way out." Robby goes to grab Jude by the arm; he's too fast and easily moves out of the way.

"Remember the last time you went to lay a finger on me? Would you like a repeat? I might have to hold you under for a few minutes to teach you a lesson," Jude goes to the cooler and takes a coke. He pops the top and takes a sip, watching us.

"Oh we're missing a couple of our friends. Let's play a game. Truth or dare? Twenty questions? You pick."

"What have you done to them?" Carrie asks.

"Alright twenty questions it is," Jude sits in a chair, while we all stand, unconsciously forming a half circle around him.

"Nothing. Next question?"

"Where are they?" I ask.

"I don't know. I'm not all knowing you know," Jude answers smugly.

"Where were they the last time you saw them?"

"In Johnny's car. At this rate, you guys aren't going to know a thing by the end of the game. I was hoping for something a little more challenging."

"Did you try and or succeed in hurting someone last night?" Seth asks.

"Yes," Jude smiles. "O. K. it's the dumb blonde guys turn, What you got for me big guy?"

"Is someone in the hospital, because of something you did?"

"Bingo. Yes. You're finally warming up. Fifteen more questions and then I gotta go. Time is short and I've got a lot to do."

"Are Johnny and Vania hurt?"

"No."

"Is someone they know hurt?"

"Yes."

Seth pipes up, "How do we get you to leave us alone?"

"You, can't, I guess you can ask . . ." Jude points to heaven.

I take a guess, "Is Vania's mom in the hospital?"

"Yes. She really shouldn't be on the road late at night especially when she's so tired from working all those hours. It really slows down the reflexes; especially when someone cuts you off and rams you into a tree."

"You guys are getting kind of boring, I quit." Jude gets up, walks to the patio door and disappears.

We grab our clothes and head to the hospital, calling information to get the number, trying to reach Vania.

Carrie tells her parents Vania's Mom had a car accident last night and we are on our way to check on her and Vania. They put lunch in the fridge and then follow us in their car. We arrive en masse.

On the ICU floor, Vania is pacing in the hallway, tears are streaming down her face. We each go up and give her a hug.

"Is your mom okay?"

"She's going to be fine, when she left work at two in the morning, she was kind of tired; she almost hit another car; then swerved off the road and hit a tree. She has a broken wrist, two cracked ribs, and her knees are cut up. They're going to release her tomorrow. They want to keep her overnight because of her head concussion. Mom was wearing her seatbelt and the air bags went off, otherwise it would've been worse."

Carrie's Mom and Dad walk up carrying some flowers. "We called Pastor Bill; he and Gina are on their way. I'm going to go in and speak to your mom and see if you can spend tonight with us, honey." Mrs. Castorelli gives Vania a hug, then goes in.

Vania talks to us, "Johnny and I were following Jude, we got held up by a red light, we came up to mom's accident right after it happened. We called 911 and had an ambulance there within minutes. Johnny went after Jude. I haven't seen him since. I hope Johnny's okay."

Robby speaks up, "Jude was just at Carrie's. He said the last time he saw Johnny, was in his car. Johnny is stronger than Jude, isn't he?" We look at each other, not sure. "He's all right, I'm sure."

Vania goes into to say goodbye to her mom. We all pile in Seth's car and he drives us back to eat our delayed lunch at Carrie's. The rest of our time goes quickly. Robby and Seth have to leave to get back tonight. Seth gives me a last hug and kiss goodbye. "Bye Megs. I don't want to leave you to face Jude without me. Robby and I will be praying for you. Leaving right now is the hardest thing I've ever done. I'm only a phone call away, okay? I love you."

"I love you too. Please be careful. I'm sure Judas is going to be targeting you and Robby too."

"I know, we'll just have to trust God to keep us safe. Maybe he'll send us an angel too, you never know."

I let Seth go. Maybe Thanksgiving, but definitely Christmas, I'll get to see him again.

After Seth leaves, the Castorellis, Vania and I head up to church for the evening service. That's where I find out where Johnny has been.

When I join my family in the pew, Max gives me a big hug. Max had been at a birthday party for his friend Trevor. Johnny is a friend of Trevor's big brother Troy. "Your friend, Johnny is really nice. He was on my team for laser tag. We came in second place." Max looks like there is something else he wants to say.

"Max what is it?"

He sees his friends from Sunday school waving him over, "Nothing." Max jumps up to go join his friends.

I have no way of getting in touch with Johnny. I guess I'll just have to wait until I see him in school.

Sunday evening, before I go to bed, my mom comes up to my room.

"Oh honey, I'm sorry, I forgot to tell you that Mandy called. She tried to reach you on your cell, but you didn't answer. I told her you were at a pool party at Carrie's with Seth."

Sure enough, I check my phone. I still had it set on vibrate and now it's dead. I plug it in and it shows six missed calls. Three from Mandy, one Seth, and two unknowns. The unknowns have me worried. Maybe Johnny called or maybe Jude called. Maybe both. I pray for a good night's sleep.

The next day at school, I wait for Carrie and Vania to show up. When Vania gets out of the car, she looks like she wants to kill someone. I catch her by the arm, "Look you can't confront Judas, he'll just make it sound like your crazy; and the teachers will believe him. With his charisma, they're deluded; they can't see Judas for what he is." I try to reason with her.

Vania won't listen. Suddenly, Johnny appears out of nowhere, directly in front of Vania. He says, "Be still."

Vania stops. She can't help herself.

"He's already defeated. Jude has lost the war; don't let him win this battle," Johnny reminds her.

Vania says, "I just want to hurt him, I want to make him pay for hurting my Mom. She's the best thing in my life." Vania starts to cry, she puts her head on Johnny's shoulder.

"It's okay. Pastor Bill saved your Mom last night; you can never be separated from her again," Vania cries and Johnny just holds her. Carrie and I rub her shoulders and say positive things. The bell rings. We walk to the front office to get excuses for running late. Carrie's mom called and let them know Vania's mom was in an accident. The school counselor has her come in to talk first, before going to any classes. Carrie says, "We'll see you at lunch, okay?" We continue to walk to our rooms.

Johnny says, "Megan, I need to talk to you."

"Yes." I think Johnny's going to give me some ideas on how to handle Vania, so what he says next floors me.

* * *

"Damon is targeting Max."

"What?"

"Max is at the age of consideration. He is coming into the knowledge of right and wrong. He is becoming aware that he has a choice to make."

"Damon is going to try and get him to reject God or take Max's life before he's saved. I'm trying to shield him from Damon's influence. I need you to persuade him how evil Damon is. I just wanted to give you a heads up. I know how much you love your little brother."

I'm stunned. How do I protect my little brother? I can't believe I have to walk into class and pretend nothing is happening. Last year I lived to go to school and get good grades. This year school seems like a huge obstacle to what's important in my life. I need to talk to Johnny on how to protect Max. He's so little. I walk into Microbiology class and ignore Jude.

At lunch, I hurry to talk to my group. I tell them what Johnny told me earlier, about Max. Mandy comes up to me in the lunchroom while we are discussing how to handle Jude's influence on Max.

"Hi, Megan."

"Hi Mandy. You looked beautiful Saturday night. Did you have a great time?"

"Oh yeah, the best. I was hoping maybe we could talk."

"Sure, why don't you give me a call tonight and we'll catch up?"

"Oh. I was hoping maybe you could come to my house or I could come to yours?"

I don't want to leave Max alone for a minute after Johnny warned me that Jude/Damon/Judas is after him. "Why don't you come to my house? I know Mom, Dad, and Max would love to see you. I'll tell them you're coming for dinner, okay?"

"Thanks," Mandy sounds relieved. Maybe she's having problems with Farrah, her mom, or Alex. Maybe she just misses me.

Vania says, "My Mom is coming home today from the hospital. Some people from the church are going to give her a ride home and they're bringing dinners for the next three nights. Isn't that sweet?" Vania continues, "Johnny's going to move into our spare room and let Mom use his car to get to and from work in the evenings, until we can get the insurance money to get the car replaced."

"Mom was worried about him having transportation," Vania giggles.

Of course being an angel, Johnny doesn't need a car to get around. He just won't be able to take us with him without the car.

Carrie says, "Johnny usually doesn't take us in the late evening anyway; I'm sure it'll be great."

Johnny speaks up, "Why is everyone talking like I'm not even here? Am I invisible or something?"

We laugh. He's the only guy in our little group and he's not even human.

I say, "Don't worry it's a girl thing."

At my afternoon math class, Jude keeps throwing gloating looks my way.

I know he's targeting someone close to me, probably besides Max.

I ignore him. Any response I have will make him target more people.

I just have to trust I will be in the right place in the right time, to stop his evil plans from happening.

After school, I meet Johnny and Vania briefly; she's excited about her Mom coming home and Johnny moving in. "I'm going to feel so much safer knowing he's here or will eventually pop up here. Judas just hates me so much. I feel like I've I had a target on my back since Jordan's death."

Things are starting to look up for Vania. Her Mom has even been given the all clear to go back to work.

Mandy is giving me a ride home today, since she's coming to my house for dinner. She pulls up in her car; I jump in and give her a hug. For once, I've put my books in a backpack. "Hey, I can't wait to hear all about your weekend on the homecoming court and your date with Alex. Tell me all about everything I've missed!" She probably had sex with Alex; it makes me sad she didn't wait. I know she was getting the message that it's okay. I hope so.

She looks happy, "Megan, I had a great weekend. Being on the court was so nice. They took our picture for the yearbook. Alex treated me like a queen. Look." Mandy shows me a gold heart necklace she's wearing with a tiny sapphire in the center. "Alex gave me his heart! Isn't that romantic?"

"Mandy, I'm happy if you're happy," I say.

She drives us the ten minutes it takes to get to my house chattering away about all the things she did and all the people she talked to at the dance. She doesn't mention what happened latter, after the dance when they went to the Hyatt. Maybe she'll want to talk about it later, in my bedroom after dinner.

Mom is so happy to see Mandy and Max is too. Last year we were as close as sisters. Mom and Max made a serve yourself taco bar with all the fixings. First Mom leads us in a prayer, then, I load up with three stuffed tacos plenty of shreded cheese and sour cream. Mandy is still watching her weight; she builds a taco salad with a small amount of meat, one crunched up shell and plenty of lettuce and tomatoes. With dinner, I see her taking two pills.

I ask, "Are you okay?"

"Yeah, I though maybe I was coming down with a cold on Thursday; I didn't want to be sick and maybe even miss homecoming, so I got a Z—Pack. Today is my last day on it. You know what the other one is," Mandy winks at me.

It's her birth control pill. I guess she followed through with her plan with Alex. We eat some blueberries for dessert; I put whip cream on mine. Mandy eats hers plain, sticking to her healthy diet. After dinner, we head up to my room.

Closing my door, we sit on my bed.

"Do you want to know how the rest of my evening went?" Mandy asks with a twinkle in her eye.

I just have to ask, "Did you do it?" "Did you and Alex, you know . . ."

Mandy plays with her necklace, "We went to the hotel; I felt so grown up you know? Alex went to the front desk and got our room key. It was a really nice room looking out over the water. There was a full moon shining on the water. We turned off the lights; it was so beautiful. We opened the sliding glass doors to the balcony and we could hear the waves breaking on the shore. He gave me this necklace out on the balcony and asked me not to break his heart. It was just like in a movie. We had a very romantic time. It hurt a little at first. I'm glad we did it. I love him and I trust him. I'm sure we'll get married someday. We're just too young right now, for marriage. We're so perfect together."

I feel bad for Mandy but I don't show it. Not too young for sex but too young for marriage? It's so backwards. I don't want to fight with her. It's not worth it and besides, it's too late now. She's made her choice.

"Alex says next time it shouldn't hurt. He's going to start coming to my house on weekends. You know my mom's always gone on her dates so she's not there anyway. Alex's parents are okay with it as long as he gets his homework done and keeps his grades up."

"Do you think you'll get engaged?" I ask.

"His parents want us to wait till he's in college next year."

I can't believe Farrah and Alex's parents are so cool about all this, I think to myself.

Mandy nods happily, "They know we're mature enough."

My parents would totally freak and forbid me to see any guy who wouldn't want to wait until marriage. They would see it as a huge sign of disrespect for me and for his own body. I don't mention any of this to Mandy now; because in the past I've already told her how I feel. She thinks my ideas are old fashioned and out of step. She knows I think her and Alex's behavior is risky.

I must look worried because Mandy says, "Don't worry, I'm taking precautions; I'm on the pill."

"What about Alex? Is he using condoms?" I ask.

Mandy blushes, "No. He says they cut down on the sensations."

"Oh."

We drop the discussion and start to talk about cheerleading, other parties she's been to, teachers and homework instead. In two weeks, on Halloween weekend, she and Alex are going to a private party being thrown by one of the cheerleaders. By the time, she leaves to go home; I realize Mandy didn't ask one question about Seth and I or how I spent my weekend or the weeks before it. I guess she thinks my life can't possibly be interesting.

Over the next two weeks, I keep an eye on Max. I watch Jude, work hard to keep up my grades and text Seth as much as possible. Vania's mom is healing and Johnny seems to have kept any mischief Jude is involved in to a minimum. Carrie has been keeping in touch with Robby and he even sent her a hermit crab for her birthday. Carrie got a big kick out of it. She even named him Robby Jr.

Carrie, Vania, Johnny and I work the trunk-or-treat on Halloween evening at our church. We have game booths set up and even turn one of the school buses into one of the scarier Bible stories. Everyone hands out candy from the trunks of their cars, it's a lot of fun. Carrie and Johnny dress up like clowns; Vania and I dress up like angels. We keep cracking up every time we look at Johnny. I guess he doesn't understand why we think that's so funny.

Monday after Halloween weekend, Mandy searches me out. She's obviously upset.

"What's wrong?" I ask.

"Janie kept flirting all night long with Alex at the Halloween party."

"Janie's the girl who threw the party right?" I ask.

"Yeah. He kept talking to her. Every time I would point out he was encouraging Janie by talking to her; he told me I was being insecure and clingy; that it was harmless. Later, when we went back to my place, I checked his phone. Her phone number was in there, so I deleted it. Now he's mad at me."

"Oh Mandy, I'm sure he'll get over it, he loves you. I point at her necklace. Just leave him alone for a day or two, give him time to miss you. I'm sure he'll call before the weekend."

I hope. I'm worried now that Mandy is no longer a challenge; maybe he is looking for his next conquest. I remember his reputation from last year.

Thursday morning, Mandy comes up to me. Her eyes are shining. "You were right, Alex called and apologized. We're getting together Friday night after the game. Thanks."

Saturday morning I get a call from Mandy, she's upset.

"Alex just went home. I don't know what to do. Last night when we went out after the game, Janie followed us. She's chasing Alex and he likes it. I don't know what to do. I'm afraid I'm going to lose him. She's making it pretty clear she would sleep with him too. I think he wants to. She keeps touching him and the way he looks at her, breaks my heart. He used to look at me that way." Mandy starts crying, "I don't know how to stop him or her. What should I do? If I stop sleeping with him, he'll just do it with her. He might any way," Mandy keeps crying.

I don't know what to tell her. If he's going to sleep around, I don't think there is any way to stop him.

"There's something else," Mandy says through her tears. "I should have gotten my period the weekend before Halloween; but it hasn't come. Megan, I think I might be pregnant."

I do some quick math. Mandy is two and a half weeks late. It's possible.

"Have you told Alex?"

"I told him this morning. He accused me of trying to trap him. He stormed out of here mad. He told me not to say anything to anyone, even if I find out I am."

"Have you told your mom, Farrah?"

"No. She's not answering her phone, which means her hot date is going well," Mandy sniffles and blows her nose.

"Okay, first we have to find out when the earliest day is that you can take a pregnancy test. Mandy, maybe your not. Maybe your body is just skipping a month from all the stress your under."

Mandy laughs sadly, "Megan I've always been regular and I've been the happiest I've ever been in my whole life. I thought Alex was the answer to my prayers," Mandy blows her nose again. "My dream is turning into a nightmare."

"Hold on Mandy," I go to my laptop and Google pregnancy test. I pull up over ten thousand sites. I narrow the search to date of ovulation to date pregnancy test can confirm.

I come up with the answer 21days. Before the hormone can for sure be detected.

"Mandy it's been 17 days; you have to wait till day 21 to be sure you don't get a false negative."

"What, what does that mean?"

"If you are pregnant, it takes that long before the hormone that shows your pregnant would show up in your urine."

"It's going to be Wednesday before we can have you take the test."

"How am I going to even buy a test? I don't want any rumors going around the school."

"Wednesday, after class, we'll drive out of town and stop at one of the big chain pharmacies. We'll do it together. What ever the answer is Mandy, you are not alone," I hang up the phone.

My worst fear for Mandy is coming true. I pray it's a false alarm. I'm mad at Farrah and at Alex's parents for being so casual about sex. I'm mad at all the TV shows where kids have sex and it's no big deal. Yet Seth and I are portrayed as the kooks.

I go downstairs to get a refill on my coffee. I go back upstairs to pray, for my friend.

Monday, I find out there was a break in at the school and computers were stolen out of the computer lab. I'm sure Jude was involved somehow. Mandy texts me she still hasn't had a visit from her friend.

Tuesday and Wednesday, I try not to think about what is happening with Mandy. I almost forget about Jude. Except for Jude purposely messing up one of our experiments in science class, he has been strangely quiet. I certainly put him on the backburner of my thoughts.

I worry about Mandy but I don't dare tell anyone. I know how these things can leak out and ruin someone's life.

Alex is acting like Mandy's caring boyfriend. Maybe he really does love her and his flirting with Janie was just a game.

Mandy comes up to me during lunch in the cafeteria, "We're still on for after school?"

"Sure," I try to smile. My stomach is tied up in knots. Alex comes over to retrieve Mandy; they certainly look happy together. Maybe everything will be okay.

I talk to Johnny, Vania and Carrie at lunch. Everything has been quiet at school. I know Johnny's been dealing with Jude after hours. He never talks about it unless it concerns us. I have a feeling a lot is going on behind the scenes. He certainly doesn't look happy most of the time.

"Johnny is there anything we can help with?" I ask.

"You're going to have your hands full soon enough."

With that ominous warning, I guess it's best to wait. I wonder if he's alluding to Mandy, Max or something I can't even imagine.

I meet Mandy out in front of the auditorium.

"What did you tell Alex?" I ask.

"I told him we were having a girl's afternoon out shopping since you and I haven't had much time together."

"So everything's okay, Janie is leaving him alone?"

Mandy says happily, "Well, Janie has started dating Drew."

I say, "Well, good, that's one less problem for you."

We start driving out of the parking lot, "Where are we heading?" I ask.

"I'm thinking ten miles north, up to Pasco County. What do you think?" Mandy asks.

"That sounds fair enough."

We avoid 'the what' if discussion and just talk about the upcoming Thanksgiving break.

"I think Seth and Robby might come down for a three day weekend."

Mandy says, "I used to be so jealous when you talked about Seth. I wanted someone to love me the way he loves you."

I don't know what to say. I'm not sure about Alex being committed to Mandy. In the next couple of hours, Mandy's whole life might change. I don't want to think about that yet.

"I hope Alex loves me enough to want to be with me forever."

"I hope so too, Mandy."

I take her hand and squeeze it before she puts it back on the steering wheel. Mandy pulls into the parking lot of one of those big 24 hour corner pharmacies. We run in and get a pregnancy test kit. We get two just in case.

As we go back to the car, I give Mandy a hug because she looks like she's about to cry. I remember how excited the newlyweds, Aaron and Regina from church were when they found out Regina was pregnant. They were so excited to tell every one in church. If Mandy's pregnant, I don't think much rejoicing is going to happen. It's awful how the same event can have such different emotional reactions.

We drive back to Mandy's house mostly in silence; each busy with our own thoughts. I'm here for moral support. Mandy can trust me to keep her private life private. As we pull into her driveway, we silently give each other another hug.

We go into the house into the bathroom. Mandy opens the box, "Here read this I'm too nervous. I can't be pregnant, I started the pill over two months ago; I know this has to be a false alarm."

I read the insert, "You have to pee on the stick for 5 seconds, no more no less. The first line that comes up is just a test line, that's the first little round window. In the second square window if two lines show up your pregnant. The second line indicates the pregnancy hormone is present."

I hand Mandy the stick, she pulls the cap off.

"Will you say a prayer with me?"

"Sure," I take her hands in mine, "Dear Lord, please let Mandy not be pregnant, please give her the chance to be a normal teenager. Amen"

I don't know what else to say, since I'm sure that even if this is a false alarm, I don't think Mandy's going to stop having sex with Alex; she's too afraid she'll lose him if she stops.

She takes the strip out, sits down and starts to pee on the stick. We both count to five. Mandy puts the stick down on the counter; her hands are shaking. She wipes and pulls up her pants.

"How long do we wait now?"

I look at the sheet, "One minute."

We both stare at the stick, watching Mandy's future.

The first line appears in the circle.

I remind her, "That's just the test line."

We both look at the square. One line appears.

A second line slowly becomes visible.

Mandy looks at me, "What does that mean?"

I show her the picture, "You are pregnant, Mandy."

I'm excited and my heart sinks at the same time.

Mandy takes the paper put of my hand and looks at the picture and at the stick, comparing the two.

"Maybe it's wrong," she says.

"Mandy, you can't have a false positive; your body is producing the pregnancy hormone."

Mandy looks at me frantically, "I can't be pregnant. I took the pill; I followed the directions exactly. That's why I got on it. My Mom even took me to get it." Mandy takes her pill pack out of the medicine cabinet and hands it to me. "There is no way I'm pregnant. The test has to be wrong. Here read this, you'll see."

I read the little insert, "Well it says one woman out of a thousand gets pregnant even if they do everything right. It also says certain drugs make the pill so it doesn't work."

Mandy looks at me funny, "What drugs?"

I look, "Antibiotics."

"Oh no," Mandy's face gets pale . . . She sits on the edge of the counter. "I took that Z-Pack the week of homecoming. I wasn't feeling well and I thought I was coming down with a cold; so I went to the doctor and got on the Z—Pack. I didn't want to miss homecoming."

"Didn't the doctor warn you?"

Mandy blushes, "I didn't tell him I was on the pill. It's none of his business. I didn't want him to know I was planning on having sex. I didn't want a lecture or the Doctor trying to talk me out of it."

We both look at the stick again. Two lines in the square. Mandy's pregnant.

Mandy looks at me, "What do I do?"

"I don't know. I guess you have to tell Alex and your Mom." I try to think of an easy way out. There isn't any.

"Do you think Alex would marry you? He is a senior and he loves you. You could get into married housing at college next year."

"He did say he loves me. Maybe we could make marriage and a baby work. Alex is coming over tonight, I'll tell him then."

I can tell Mandy is afraid to face Alex.

"Megan, could you come over, please, around seven thirty? Please? I know I should tell Alex privately. But maybe you can tell him some of these things. I'm so nervous, I'm afraid I'll forget."

I nod my head yes, and give her a hug.

"I know he isn't going to be happy at first, but I think he loves me enough to marry me," Mandy smiles, "It doesn't have to be the end of the world does it?"

"When are you going to tell your mom, Farrah?" I ask.

"Not till after I tell Alex, if we're going to get married, we can face my mom together, and his parents too."

Mandy gives me a ride home before dinner. She needs some time to think of how she's going to break the news to Alex. I ask my Mom to please drop me off at Mandy's, after dinner, on her way to Max's karate class. She agrees.

I say a prayer that things work out for Alex and Mandy. I'll know soon enough when I see her later tonight. On the way to Mandy's house, I'm nervous and feeling nauseous. I can't believe this is happening. Mandy and I had a plan. We were going to go to college together, share an apartment and have fun. Now my best friend might be getting married and have a baby, a family.

My mom drops me off and gives me a kiss, "Have fun honey, tell Mandy to stop by more often; we miss her."

"I will, love you Mom, love you, Max, have fun at karate."

I walk up to the front door. Alex's car is still in the driveway. I stand there for a minute, unsure if I should ring the bell. I hear yelling and screaming. Unfortunately, it sounds like things are not going well. I feel so bad for Mandy. I don't want to intrude, but Mandy might need my support as a friend. I get the courage up to ring the bell. I hear low voices and then hear Mandy say through the closed door, "she already knows."

Mandy opens the door, she's been crying and her face is red with traces of smeared mascara. "Come in."

Alex is standing in the living room, pacing back and forth.

"Look Mandy told me, you know; so far it's only us three."

Mandy talks to me, ignoring Alex for the moment. "He didn't believe me when I told him I was pregnant. He thought I was faking it, to trap him. He made me take the second pregnancy test and pee in front of him! Then, he accused me of sleeping with somebody else." Mandy dissolves in tears against my shoulder.

Alex obviously doesn't want to yell in front of me. "Look Mandy, we're too young to get married. We haven't even gotten through high school yet. And our best years are a head of us in college. I'm not ready to be a dad and you don't want to be a mom; come on honey," He walks up behind Mandy and starts rubbing her arms, "We can get this taken care of, I'll pay of course, the sooner we get this taken care of, the better."

Mandy turns to him, "What are you saying? That you want to get married and you'll pay for the license?"

Alex looks at her, "Don't be stupid. You have to get an abortion. I'm not paying child support and we are not getting married. If we do it now, quietly, our parents don't even have to know." Alex looks directly at me, "No one has to know."

"Don't ruin my senior year of high school; Mandy, if you love me, you'll get it now. The clinics are closed tonight. We'll call first thing tomorrow and set up an appointment."

Mandy's crying, "Alex it's a baby, our baby, I can't kill it. We could get married and live in student housing next year; you can still go to college. It won't be easy, but we can do it. Other people do."

Alex looks at Mandy coldly, "It's a blob of cells, an accident, because you were to dumb to follow instructions. You want me to sacrifice my life for the next 18 years for your mistake. How can you be so selfish?"

Alex picks up the phone and dials information. "Clearwater, Florida,"

We hear him say to the automated attendant. "Abortion clinic" The machine can't understand him so he repeats his request to a live operator, "Abortion clinic."

He writes the number down on a piece of paper and hangs up the phone.

"You call tomorrow and make the appointment or I will." He thrusts the piece of paper with the number on it at Mandy. "We are taking care of this mistake before anyone else finds out."

Alex looks at me one last time before he walks out the door, "You better keep your mouth shut," he leaves.

I hold Mandy as we sit down on the couch and I just let her cry.

"What am I going to do? What should I do Megan?"

I don't know what to say. I believe abortion is murder. I tell Mandy, "You know what I believe," we've had this discussion before.

"What are my choices if I have the baby? Keep it? I don't want to be a mom all by myself and Alex doesn't want to help. Put the baby up for adoption and let some stranger raise it? Maybe abortion is the best solution."

I get a little mad at her logic.

"You're right, murdering the baby is better than letting a stranger love your baby and raise it."

Mandy starts to cry again, "You don't have to be so cruel."

I look at her and say, "This is a real human being growing in you. You can't just think of yourself anymore. You have to think of your baby's future too. Mandy you have to grow up and think of what's best for the baby."

Mandy looks at the piece of paper in her hand with the abortion clinic's phone number on it. I'm afraid to suggest Mandy talk to her mom. Farrah goes out and parties, sleeps around with men and gets drunk almost every night. I'm afraid she'll tell Mandy abortion is okay the same way she told her being on birth control and having sex is okay.

"I would really like you to talk to my Pastor and his wife about this; they can help you," I say.

Mandy wipes at her eyes, "No, thank you. I don't need any one to make me feel worse than I already do. I don't need lectures; I need help."

She looks at me, "Megan I know abortion is wrong, I just honestly don't want to face everything alone. My mom's too busy partying to care. I can't see her being any help at all. Please don't tell anyone. I won't make a decision tonight. I promise."

I can't leave Mandy alone tonight, without anyone to talk to. I make a snap decision and announce, "I'm spending the night tonight; I can't leave you alone."

"Really? Thank you Megan. You're the best," Mandy sounds re-lieved. I give her a hug.

I call my mom to let her know I'm going to be spending the night at Mandy's. Mandy can drive me to my house before school, that way I can change clothes and pick up my books. My cell rings, after I hang up with my mom. The number says 'private'. It could be Johnny; or it could be Jude. I hesitate before I answer. I'm afraid of who it might be.

"Surprise! A bun in the oven. Isn't this the best? I get a mother and a father to commit murder and a dead baby. Three more for me. I call this a triple crown. Just like the good old days with Adrammelech and Anam-melech.[55] I just love surprises! I almost spilled the beans once or twice. It's so hard to keep secrets. Especially from you, mouse. No wonder you humans fail at it so often. My mouse, my pet, my toy." His voice keeps changing as he talks, sounding like the demon he is.

"Why don't I come over and make Mandy feel better about aborting. I won't even tell any one; maybe, maybe I won't tell anyone. But it's so hard to keep secrets; I don't know . . . maybe you can talk me out of tell-ing, mouse. Oh, I almost forgot why I called. Give Max my best. I haven't seen the little bugger lately. Where have you been hiding him? Oh, I get it, we're playing hide and seek. What fun!"

With that, the phone clicks off. I'm worried about Max, but I have a chance of saving Mandy and her baby. Max is safe at home with Mom and Dad. I can't worry about him tonight. Besides, I'm afraid Jude is using Max as a distraction so I don't concentrate on saving Mandy's baby. Man-dy assumes the call was from my mom checking up on me, so she went ahead with getting sheets to cover the couches. We'll spend the night out in the living room. It's bigger and more comfortable than Mandy's room. We plan to watch a movie.

Farrah comes home three or four hours after the movie is over. We're both sleeping. I vaguely hear her getting ready for bed in my light sleep.

Suddenly the lights come on, "Get UP. Get Up now, both of you." My eyes are blurry from trying to focus while I'm still half-asleep.

Farrah is standing at the end of Mandy's couch where she can see us both clearly.

"Which one of you is it? Which one?" Farrah is shaking. She looks angry and upset. I realize she's holding up the pregnancy test kit stick.

Mandy is still rubbing the sleep from her eyes. I just look between her and Farrah. I'm totally paralyzed by fear. I know I haven't done any-thing wrong, but I feel like we've been caught doing something bad.

"It's me, Mom, stop yelling," Mandy sits up while Farrah sits down on the edge of Mandy's couch. "I have had enough yelling from Alex. I was going to tell you tomorrow, I mean later this morning; I just found out myself."

"Oh honey," Farrah reaches out to Mandy and starts crying. Farrah must still be a little drunk. Her reactions are a little over the top and she is slurring her words slightly.

"What did Alex say?" Farrah asks.

"He wants me to have an abortion." Farrah's face crumples and she starts to cry. "I'm so sorry baby, I'm so sorry." She holds on to Mandy and rocks her back and forth, saying, as if it's a mantra, "I'm so sorry, I'm so sorry."

It's such a personal moment, I'm afraid to remind anybody I'm here. I just lie back down.

It's almost like Mandy is the one comforting her mother. She starts soothing Farrah by saying, "It's okay Mom, it's okay don't cry."

I slowly get up and move into Mandy's bedroom to give them some privacy. After awhile I fall asleep. I didn't think I could, but when I open my eyes, it's morning.

# Chapter Ten

## Decision Time

Thursday morning, I go out to the kitchen and start a pot of coffee, I know where everything is, Mandy I have been friends for so long. I wake Mandy up to remind her we have to leave to go to my house and then school after.

Mandy comes into the kitchen. "I'm going to call in sick today."

"Why?" I ask. I pour myself a cup of coffee and sit down at the table.

"I'm going to call the clinic and schedule an abortion as soon as they open."

"Mandy, don't, you told me you know it's wrong; you can't." I say shocked.

"Come on, you saw my Mom's reaction last night. I can't take care of her and a baby."

"Mandy please, let's talk to my Pastor, there are groups out there that help girls. Please let's talk to one of them first, I beg."

"No, Alex was right. The less people who know the better," Mandy starts to pour a cup of coffee then stops. She lets out a laugh, and starts to pour again.

Mandy turns to me, "I almost stopped pouring the coffee because I thought it's bad for the baby." She starts to cry.

I go up and hug her. "Mandy you could keep the baby or you could put the baby up for adoption. I've heard you can even pick out the adoptive family if you want. I've heard that some of the families will even send you pictures as your child grows up. Please let's go talk to someone."

"No, I know what I have to do," Mandy dries her tears, picks up the phone and dials.

I can't believe anyone would be there this early. I pray they are not open yet.

Mandy says, "Hello, I would like to schedule an appointment for today, as soon as possible. Where exactly are you?" She writes down an address.

"Ten o'clock, that will be fine. Thank you."

She hangs up and looks at me. "There it's done. I'm going to drive over to Alex's house now to get his credit card to pay for it. I'm going to leave now before I change my mind. Alex will drop me off at the clinic. I'll call him when it's over and he can give me a ride home. By Monday, we can pretend this never happened and things can go back to normal. Don't make a big deal out of this, Megan," Mandy gets up. "I have to get changed."

Mandy goes to get ready.

* * *

I just sit in shock. I can't believe this is happening. I can't believe how easy it is to get an abortion. I can see Mandy changing already in front of my eyes.

I look at the name and address of the clinic. Crisis Pregnancy Center, 5300 Hwy. 19 N.

I don't know what to do. I can't go to school; I'm to upset. I don't know who I can talk to that could change Mandy's mind. Please God give me a way, show me a way to save her baby. I know if Mandy goes through with this, she'll be changed forever. She can't even watch nature shows with out crying every time some animal dies.

I hear Mandy in the shower. I can't move for fear that I'm going to throw up. I'm afraid to wake Farrah because I think she'll be all for Mandy getting an abortion. I get on the phone and call information for my pastor's number. It's early and he doesn't pick up. Maybe he's in the shower. I leave a quick message asking him to pray for Mandy and what she plans to do.

When Mandy comes out, I tell her, "I'm coming with you."

"No you're not, this is between Alex and me," she looks at me blankly, all emotion gone.

"Nothing you can say will change my mind. Please don't judge me until you've walked in my shoes."

I feel this is my last chance to get through to her, the horror of what she's about to do.

"Mandy, I'm not judging, my heart is so sad, for you and the baby." Tears start running down my face.

"You, Mom, Alex and I are the only ones who know. Let's keep it that way? Okay?" Mandy picks up her car keys and heads out the door. I hear her drive away. I've never seen her so empty before, so hopeless.

I sit there in shocked silence and begin to pray. About an hour latter, I hear Farrah getting up and getting ready. She comes into the kitchen looking beautiful as always.

"Hi Megan, where's Mandy? Is she still sleeping?" Farrah pours herself a cup of coffee. "Can you go wake her? I really need to talk to her."

I look at her and say, "She's left."

"Left? She went to school without you? That doesn't make any sense."

"No." I say sounding defeated almost in tears. "She went to Alex's house to pick up his credit card, and then he's driving her to the clinic to get an abortion." I start to cry.

Farrah drops her mug and hot coffee explodes everywhere in the tiny kitchen. Some of it lands on my jeans, but I don't care.

"No. This can't be happening. Do you know where she went? Tell me where she went!"

Farrah steps on pieces of the broken mug with her bare feet to get to me; she's in a panic and she doesn't notice she's getting cut up.

"It's a clinic, off of Hwy 19. She has an appointment at ten o'clock." We look at the clock it's ten minutes after ten.

"Get in the car," Farrah says as she puts flip-flops on her bleeding feet. "Oh God. I hope we're not too late," The way she's says it, it almost sounds like a prayer.

We get in the car and start to drive; we are only about 10 minutes away.

Farrah keeps saying over and over, "Please God don't let us be too late."

I pray the same thing silently with her.

We arrive at the clinic. Above the door it says, 'Crisis Pregnancy Center.' I'm afraid to go in; I'm afraid of what it will smell like. I remember the scent of the dead frogs soaked in formaldehyde in science class. That's what my brain tells me I'm going to smell. The coffee I drank on an empty stomach fights to come back up. Farrah opens the door and pushes me inside. I'm afraid to breathe; I almost pass out as I walk in.

The lady at the reception desk gives us a warm smile and hands us an intake form. "Here fill this out. Are you here for a pregnancy test?" She smiles at me. I take a breath. It smells nice, like lavender.

"We're here for Mandy, my daughter. She had a ten o'clock appointment. Is she back there somewhere? I have to see her," Farrah tries to smile. It looks more like a grimace.

The counselor smiles at her and motions her to sit down, "Our clients have a right to privacy; we can't give that information out."

Farrah looks shocked, "But I'm her mother and she's underage."

"She still has the right to privacy; I'm sorry, but it's the law," the counselor says.

Farrah gets up and pushes her way past the counselor, heading to the door that leads toward the back, she yells at the top of her lungs, "Mandy!" "Mandy, it's your mom, you answer me now. Mandy where are you? Mandy please don't get an abortion, sweet heart, please answer me, I'm here, Mandy please, Mommy's here!"

Farrah sounds frantic as she continues down the hall. A door, three doors down from where we are standing, opens and there is Mandy, standing in the doorway. Farrah runs to her, encircles her in a big hug crying, "Oh baby, its okay, please, oh please, don't do it; don't make the same mistake I did. Don't kill your baby. I don't want you to suffer the way I have all these years. Don't kill your baby like I did." Farrah sobs.

The counselor comes out and puts her hand on Farrah's shoulder, "It's okay, God forgives you. You don't have to live with the guilt anymore."

The counselor takes them both into the room and shuts the door. I hear both Farrah and Mandy crying their hearts out.

The counselor we pushed past gently taps me on the shoulder and gestures me out to the main waiting room. It's then that I notice for the first time, the pictures of the baby fetuses on the wall. They're framed showing the different stages of development. I also notice the scriptures from the Bible. "I knit you together in your mother's womb." "I knew you before you were born."[56] "You are fearfully and wonderfully made."[57]

I turn to the counselor, "You're not an abortion clinic are you?"

She smiles, "No. We're not."

"But I don't get it, my friend called for an abortion clinic and they gave her your number."

She smiles again, "It's not the first time this has happened. God does work in mysterious ways."

I sit out front and notice all the literature on the table; it's in English and Spanish. The pamphlets are all about STD's, pregnancies, marriage, abstinence, parenting skills, life skills how to get your GED, how to finish high school, internet college classes, job training, and adoption.

"My name is Amy. I'm a volunteer counselor here."

"I'm Megan."

The counselor looks at me and asks, "Is that your mom and sister back there?"

"No. That's my best friend and her mom. I hope you can talk her out of getting an abortion."

Amy smiles, "We do more than just that. We don't want Mandy to have the baby and then abandon her to have even more problems than she has now. We'll see Mandy through her whole pregnancy, get her into a good Bible based church which will 'adopt' her and show Mandy unconditional love; this way even if she doesn't have a supportive family, she can have a church family. We'll help Mandy finish her education, get a career, or apply to colleges, get grants and qualify her for government programs that help young women just like her. If she chooses to put the baby up for adoption, we will help Mandy find a loving family to take the baby. If she chooses to keep her baby, we offer parenting classes and life skill classes. We can get her job training or apprenticeships, and direct her to good day care programs. The choices are endless. Our door is always open."

Amy points to a wall. It's covered with pictures of babies and toddlers. "These are the babies we've helped; each one represents a mother we've helped too."

"If your friend decides to go through with her abortion, we offer after care counseling. Many women who make that decision find they can't live with it and turn later in life to alcohol or drugs. We offer counseling to help them get over the guilt."

"I had no idea you guys we're even here."

Amy nods her head, "We don't get any government funding, unlike Planned Parenthood or other programs that offer abortion or birth control. Mostly we're run by volunteers and supported by groups of churches."

Amy asks, "Would you like to pray for your friend?"

"Yes, I would," we clasp hands and Amy guides us in a prayer asking God to touch Mandy's heart and give her peace.

I feel at peace. I've done everything that I can. The rest is up to God. If Mandy decides to carry her baby to term, I'll be here for her. I hope that's the choice she makes. I know the next nine months will be hard for her and she'll need me as a friend.

My phone rings. The screen says private. I don't want to answer fearful of hearing Jude's taunting again, but I do just in case it's Johnny.

"Hi Megan," I breathe a sigh of relief. It's Johnny.

"I think everything's going to be okay with Mandy and her mom," I say. I feel hopeful.

"Say a prayer though for your little brother."

"My brother, what do you mean?" I ask. Oh, no, what has Jude done? My heart so at peace just a minute ago, starts to sink.

"Stay there; I'm coming to pick you up," Johnny says.

Suddenly my Mom is on the phone, I can hear the panic in her voice. "Honey, Max didn't make it to school this morning. He's missing," my heart drops.

I remember Judas/Jude/Damon's threatening call last night, the one about hide and seek. There's no doubt in my mind Jude has taken my little brother. Johnny knows it too. I hope he has some ideas of where Jude's taken him, places where we can look.

"Mom, Johnny's on his way to pick me up; don't worry, we'll find him." I try to sound confident.

She continues, "The police won't put out an amber alert for him for a couple of hours, because they think maybe he's just skipping school. They think he'll come home on his own."

"Don't worry Mom, we'll find him, he's a smart kid. I'm sure he'll show up soon." I don't believe it for one minute. Jude's deadly game is on, this time involving my own brother. It's my turn to seek. I guess it's my turn, my only chance, to find my little brother, before it's too late.

THE END

**Don't miss the second book in the angel series, *Angel in the Storm.***

King James Bible Footnotes to follow on next page.

# Notes

[1] Gen. 28:12, Hosea 12:4, Matt. 2:13, 2 Cor. 11:14
[2] Heb. 1:14, Rev. 12:7
[3] Heb. 1:14, Ps. 91:11, Rom. 12:6–8
[4] Matt. 10:34, Rev. 12:7–9, Rev. 12:12
[5] Matt. 10:28, 1 Pet. 5:8, Job 1:6–12
[6] Eph. 6:10–18, Rom. 13:12
[7] John 7:16–17, John 8:12, Deut. 30:19
[8] Eph. 6:12, 2 Cor. 2:11, Jude 1:22–23
[9] Matt. 13:37–43, Jude 1:25
[10] Ps. 46:10
[11] Mark 10:14, Matt. 19:14
[12] 1 Sam. 17:42–50
[13] John 3:20–21
[14] Job 2:10, Prov. 24:10, Ps. 119:50
[15] Eph. 6:18, 1 Thess. 5:17, James 5:13, Phil. 4:6
[16] Mat 4:5–11
[17] Eph 6:17, Heb 4:12
[18] 2 Pet. 2:11
[19] Gen. 28:12, Rev. 12:7–9, Job 1:6–7
[20] Rev. 12:9, John 12:31
[21] Luke 22:31, Job 1:12, Heb. 12:6–7, 10–11
[22] Col. 2:18–19, Heb. 1:6
[23] Ps. 16:9, Phil. 4:4–7, Eccles. 11:9
[24] Heb. 8:5, Col. 2:17
[25] Rev. 5:11–12, Heb. 12:22–23, Heb. 1:6
[26] 1 Pet. 5:8–9
[27] Luke 8:12
[28] Exod. 23:20, Ps. 34:7
[29] Mark 9:29
[30] 1 Pet. 1:2
[31] 2 Pet. 3:9

[32] James 5:20, 1 Pet. 5:8–9

[33] James 2:19, James 4:7, 2 Pet. 2:10–12

[34] Rev. 12:7

[35] 1 Pet. 5:8

[36] Matt. 16:18, Rev. 1:18, Rev. 20:14, Matt. 5:29–30

[37] Rom. 3:23

[38] Luke 13:5, Acts 2:38, John 3:16

[39] John 17:5, John 17:1–25

[40] NIV Isa. 40:6–8, 1 Pet. 1:24

[41] 1 Pet. 5: 8

[42] Luke 22:31

[43] Matt. 6:25–27

[44] Gen. 17:5, Gen. 17:15

[45] Gen. 29:35

[46] Rom. 3:23, Rom. 3:10

[47] Mark 1:4, Luke 5:31–32, Rom. 2:4

[48] Rom. 6:23

[49] John 3:16, 1 Pet. 3:21, Titus 3:7, 1 John 2:25, 1 John 5:13, Jude 1:21

[50] Acts 15:11, 1 Cor. 15:2, Rom.1:4–9

[51] Luke 15:7

[52] Heb. 1:14

[53] Mark 5:9, John 8:44

[54] John 10:36

[55] 2 Kings 17:31

[56] Jer. 1:5, Deut. 32:6

[57] Ps. 139:14

Breinigsville, PA USA
14 April 2010
236162BV00003B/8/P